Justine decided she'd had too much sun

"I'd best get indoors," she told Wyatt.

"Easier to apply some sunscreen," he countered. "I'll put it on for you."

"I think not," she hedged, but before she could object further, she felt the lotion being dribbled down her back. Then strong yet somehow delicate fingers were at work spreading the lotion across her shoulders.

Wyatt's fingers had a tantalizing eroticism to them as they alternately caressed and massaged her. She half reared up when an unexpected tug released the string of her bikini, but as quickly realized she couldn't get up—not now.

"I wish you'd stop," she told him.

"Stop what? This?" And his fingers traced a tingling line down her spine, then circled in a spiral, following the white line left by the bikini strings, toward the swelling of her breasts.

Dinner at Wyatt's

by

VICTORIA GORDON

Harlequin Books

TORONTO • NEW YORK • LOS ANGELES • LONDON
AMSTERDAM • PARIS • SYDNEY • HAMBURG
STOCKHOLM • ATHENS • TOKYO • MILAN

Original hardcover edition published in 1982
by Mills & Boon Limited

ISBN 0-373-02531-9

Harlequin Romance first edition February 1983

CHAPTER ONE

JUSTINE rubbed her palms nervously along the sides of her skirt and tried to swallow the knot that seemed to have boiled into a solid lump in her throat. As she stood outside her small car, the house—the *restaurant*, she corrected herself—looked so much more imposing than when she'd driven up the long, curving approach road. A sign, dark blue on a discreet pale blue background, proclaimed **Wyatt's** in a strong, bold script. Justine took a slow, deep breath and muttered to herself, 'Come on, stop fiddling about and get on with it! Even if it is your first job as head chef, you can't stand out here dithering all morning.'

The thought of anyone seeing her, shifting from foot to foot like a punch-drunk fighter, brought a wry smile to her lips and somehow broke the inertia. She moved briskly up the broad stone steps to the front door of the establishment. It took another deep breath before she finally put out one trembling hand and pushed open the carved oaken panels that gleamed with polish and care. After the heat and sunlight outside, the cool, sophisticated interior of the foyer was more than welcome and Justine looked about her with uninhibited curiosity.

The dark and light blue motif was obviously the major colour scheme, for a pale carpet stretched out ahead of her, meeting a wide staircase at the end of the long hallway. A narrower strip of similar carpet led to the right of the stair case, into a pool of shadow.

Probably leads to a cloakroom, though I wouldn't envy anybody having to work back in that gloom, she thought. The mental picture she got was of dark and dwarfish creatures skulking about with the heavy tweeds and minks that patrons of such an establishment might shed before dining. She snorted aloud at the thought, a small sound that was swallowed without echo in the cavernous maw of soft carpeting and pale, polished wood panels.

'Who's that?' came a sharp question from her right in a voice that slashed like a dagger through the softness of the atmosphere, and Justine wheeled nervously, her eyes searching through the archway that opened on a small, intimate dining salon. Facing her was a tall, lean figure, features hidden in the back-lit gloom. Her immediate impression was of a poised rapier, a weapon alert and ready for instant action.

'Good . . . morning,' she said, fighting for calmness in her voice. 'I'm looking for Mr Wyatt Burns.'

The man, his face and features still shadowed by the effect of light silhouetting him from behind, replied sharply. 'You've got him,' he said, and Justine shivered at the coldness in his voice.

'I'm . . . Justine Ryan, Mr Burns,' she said after a long, expectant silence.

'So?'

'So?' she repeated his question, then said, 'Your new chef?'

'The hell you are!' The words ripped from him with explosive force and he stalked three tigerish steps towards her with such evident menace that Justine shrank back against the opposite wall.

Then she took hold of herself and her failing courage, lifting her head to glare back at this haughty, insolent man. 'In your own words, the hell I *am*,' she snapped. 'Although I must admit I expected a somewhat more gracious welcome. The tone of your letter certainly didn't indicate any such animosity—or is this simply your idea of being the boss?'

'Boss!' The word was accompanied by a barely-disguised oath as he strode forward to stand squarely before her, staring down like an avenging angel. Justine was now further at a disadvantage, since the light from behind him now struck her squarely in the eyes and his features were lost in a blur of light-haze.

An impatient sigh gusted from him. 'You'd better come up to the office, I think,' he growled, turning away and moving swiftly towards the stairs. Justine stood for a moment in confusion, until his grating voice floated across to her. 'Now, if you don't mind!'

Her eyes readjusted as she turned away from the direct light, and she found herself watching the broad shoulders and long, muscular legs of the man as he seemed to fly up the staircase. Then he stopped and glared back at her with obvious impatience.

'I'm coming ... I'm coming,' Justine snapped furiously, and suited actions to words by hurrying towards the stairs. It wasn't difficult to keep the tall, angry figure in view as it strode ahead of her up the carpeted staircase and then down a hall to where huge double doors filled the end of the hallway from floor to twelve-foot-high ceiling. One of them opened smoothly and Wyatt Burns stood aside in a parody of good manners, ushering her into a large room that was light and airy with floor-to-ceiling windows opened to the spicy summer air.

Justine had time for one quick sweep of the room before her eyes were drawn to the saturnine face that stared bleakly at her from across half an acre of walnut desk-top. Wyatt Burns, she thought, had features that suited the crystalline chillness of his voice. Black hair, black eyes, the dark line of beard shadow along his jaw merging to a harsh-planed face that was dark as the desk-top. Every aspect of his carriage shouted a jungle fierceness, a vivid masculinity held only just in check. He had dropped into a huge winged chair behind the desk, but made no offer of a seat to Justine.

Her eyes narrowed a touch and she tilted her chin before moving smoothly into a soft armchair directly opposite his, dropping her handbag and crossing her legs neatly before meeting his chilly stare. Wyatt

Burns' dark eyes seemed bottomless as they first met
her glance, then roved casually over her body, appraising with frank regard her long legs and the curves of a
slim body beneath her two-piece cheesecloth summer
suit.

One sooty eyebrow was raised in . . . was it approval
or disdain? she wondered . . . before his lips flickered
into what could only be considered a sneer.

Justine allowed herself no obvious reaction; only her
eyes revealed the growing anger inside her. They were,
she knew, a sparkling emerald green, reflecting her
mood of the moment without any intimation that in
other moods they could shift from blue for happiness
to grey for uncertainty or sadness.

This man's eyes held no such flexibility, she
thought, but would be that same hot charcoal hue
whether angry or in the throes of other passions.
Suddenly she realised that he'd been speaking while
her thoughts had wandered, but she caught only the
final words, '. . . false pretences.'

'*What?*What false pretences?' she demanded, sitting up
abruptly. What was this arrogant person talking about?

A dark and biting glance took in her furious face,
and she fancied he was truly enjoying the confrontation. 'The false pretences,' he said deliberately, 'that
you employed to get yourself hired here, despite
knowing I wouldn't have a female chef on the
premises!' He spat out the final words with a sneer of
frank distaste.

Justine's jaw dropped. Stunned, she could only stare
at him in silence, until finally he sneered, 'Cat got your
tongue, *Miss* Ryan?'

'Why, you . . .' Justine spluttered, then hauled in a
deep breath as she grabbed for the remnants of her
tattered composure. In a rigid, controlled voice, she
said carefully, 'I had no idea that you were so set
against female chefs, *Mr* Burns, or I would never have
bothered to reply to your advertisement. Since I did,

however, and since I'm obviously female, why on earth did you hire me in the first place?' She couldn't control the slight softening of inflection as she continued, 'Oh, I know I never actually stated my sex one way or another in my letter of application, but I certainly wouldn't have thought with a name like Justine ...' She faltered there at the mocking sneer on his face.

'Very clever,' he retorted. 'Excellent explanation, despite you knowing damned well why I didn't pick up your sex straight away.' He flicked his wrist and a sheet of paper fluttered over the desk to sail down at her feet. She bent to retrieve it, suddenly all too conscious of the gaping neckline of her suit as she did so.

It was, as she'd half suspected, her letter of application for the job at Wyatt's, but a quick perusal brought her no closer to understanding than she'd been before.

'I don't understand,' she said uncertainly.

Silence.

'Well?' Her voice squeaked childishly and she winced.

'Well? Well, *look* at it!' he snarled. 'How many people do you know that would spell Justine as Justin—*e*?'

Justine's eyes flew back to the page, only to lift again in horror. Her ineffectual typing had finally caught up with her. Colour flooded her face as the mocking voice taunted her.

'I thought all I was in for was a slightly mad chef who had peculiar ideas about how he wanted his name and initial on the pay cheque,' Wyatt Burns snorted. 'But what do I get instead? A blushing blonde female!' Contempt dripped from his voice like acid, stinging Justine to fury.

'I'm a chef, not a typist!' she stormed, glaring across the desk as if looks could kill. 'You ought to be damned well pleased that I even bothered to type the application in the first place!' As she stopped for a much-needed breath, a sudden thought occurred to her. 'Didn't you even check out my references? Surely to goodness my last employer would have told you I was female?'

Wyatt had the grace to stop sneering, but he didn't seem ready to accept her questions. 'I did,' he said, 'but with that atrocious pseudo-French accent, Justine and Justin are pretty damned close. Your femininity didn't come into the discussion because it hadn't occurred to me, and personally I doubt if it ever occurred to him, either.'

'Well, that's true enough,' she muttered, 'but none-theless, I certainly didn't set out to deceive you—al-though,' and her anger was growing again, fanned by his insolence, 'I don't much care, either. So if that's it, I'm off. You can take your damned job and shove it where it'll do you the most good—sideways!'

Grabbing up her handbag, she leapt from the chair as if it was on fire, and actually had her hand on the doorknob before his voice cracked out like a whiplash to stop her.

'Come back here and sit down,' he snapped. Justine stopped, half turned, then turned fully to face him, her eyes bleak.

'I don't think so,' she replied coldly. 'I think I've listened to quite enough chauvinistic rubbish for one day. If I leave now I can be back in Sydney in time to start looking for a job. You and I have nothing left to discuss.'

'I disagree,' he said, uncoiling from his chair and moving to stand only inches in front of her, eyes flow-ing across her heavy coronet of strawberry-blonde hair.

Then his eyes met hers again, and his dark brows drew together in a quizzical frown. 'How tall are you?' he asked abruptly, and the irrelevance of the question startled her.

'Five foot ten,' she replied without thinking, then

realised just how far up she was forced to look in order to meet his daunting black eyes.

They seemed warmer, somehow, though still speculative, and she found herself wondering if she dared throw the same question back at him. The thought brought a tiny quirk to one corner of her lips.

'A hundred and ninety-six centimetres,' he replied soberly, not waiting for the question but suddenly grinning hugely at the look on her face. 'That's six foot five—and yes, I was reading your mind. It wasn't that difficult.'

Before she could think, he had taken her arm and gently led her to where a plush settee filled the alcove between two sets of bay windows.

'Sit down,' he said gently. 'Can I get you a drink?'

Justine shook her head mutely. The last thing she needed at this precise moment was a drink, but when he asked if she minded him having one, she merely shook her head again.

Three ice cubes and a splash of expensive whisky tinkled into a thick glass, and she found herself thinking how much the drink suited him. No fancy cocktail drinker, this man. Tall, dark and devilish, with a strong, thick neck, massive shoulders, yet astonishingly slender hips, he didn't look gangly or unfinished as so many really tall men do, nor yet gigantic or clumsy. He moved ... economically. Like a great cat, she thought, and suddenly found he had turned to find her watching him, appraising him.

Something flashed briefly in his eyes, but his voice was butter-smooth and suave when he drifted over to sit beside her, glass in hand. 'Now, Justine,' he said softly, accenting the final *e* in her name, 'why have you so definitely decided you don't want to work for me?'

Justine stared, wordless. The unexpected phrasing of the question had taken her by surprise. A puzzled frown furrowed her forehead and she licked her full lips as she struggled for a reply.

'I thought it was rather the other way round,' she said finally. 'I wanted to work here or I wouldn't have applied. It wasn't me who decided I'm not suitable.'

She looked down then, waiting vainly for a reply as her eyes focused on the long, lean fingers that curled like talons around the glass. When he didn't reply, she continued without looking up.

'And since you made your position clear—abundantly clear—I don't quite see why you asked me that question.'

He sipped at the drink, the lifting of the glass bringing her eyes up with it until he could lock her glance with his own as his tongue moved idly around the rim of the glass. It was a slow, deliberately sensual motion that quite matched the look in his eye.

'Maybe I've changed my mind,' he said carelessly. And as she flashed astonishment with her eyes, his lips parted in a glimmering smile. 'It's not only a feminine prerogative, you know.'

Amusement crinkled his eyes, altering his expression totally. He looked . . . almost boyish, Justine found to her surprise.

'Your application was the best I received,' he told her. 'I need a head chef and I need one immediately; the incumbent left yesterday and tomorrow we've got virtually a full house expected.' He swirled the shrinking islands of ice in his glass, staring at them meditatively before continuing, 'So I propose to give you a month's trial. That should settle the matter one way or the other, and give me time to find somebody else if you decide not to stay. Agreed?'

Too smooth, too suave, too easy. Justine's temper slipped its controls as she flew to her feet, grabbing up her handbag on the way.

'Well, thanks a lot!' she cried. 'All you're looking for, Mr Wyatt Burns, is a fill-in to carry you until you've found the male chef you wanted in the first place. Anybody could do that job, but not me! Nooo

way! I came all the way out here in good faith to take a
job I rightfully believed I'd been hired for and which
I know damned well I can do to the satisfaction of any
reasonable employer. I have absolutely no intention of
providing you with nuisance value for a month while
you're busy advertising behind my back to get the
person you really want!'

On that note, she stormed full steam ahead for the
door, only to find herself restrained on the threshold
by steely fingers that clamped round her upper arm
like a vice. Wyatt Burns swung her back to face him,
his face dark with barely-suppressed anger.

'I would *not* be advertising behind your back,' he
growled. 'And I was not—repeat, not—looking at you as
somebody to fill in, as you put it. I offered you a
month's trial exactly as I would have offered it to
anyone else under the circumstances. Anyone else—
male or female or neuter. If you'd managed to keep
that childish temper of yours under control long
enough to try my offer, you'd have found soon
enough that it's a condition all of my staff have
endured.'

Whereupon he released her arm disdainfully, indeed
with a gesture that conveyed only a distaste, as if he'd
picked up a toad and found it slimy. Then he turned
on his heel and stalked back into his office, shutting
the door quietly but firmly behind him.

Justine stood, shaken, on the top of the stairs, rather
astonished at the directness of his charges. Childish?
Well, maybe. Certainly she had a quick temper, and at
twenty-six she was wise enough to realise it. And, she
admitted ruefully, usually wise enough also to control
it. Still, there had been a ring of truth in Wyatt Burns'
final words. But I was just as truthful, she cried silently
and belligerently, only to find her truculence fading
and slowly being replaced by a sense of guilt. Perhaps
she had misjudged him. The way he'd explained it,
with her own poor typing to back up his claim, perhaps

he should be forgiven for being surprised and annoyed at finding she was female.

Moreover, she did want to work at Wyatt's. So before she could give herself time to change her mind or do anything foolish, she turned back to the forbidding office door, tapped lightly on it with her fingernails, and stepped inside without waiting for a summons.

'Good morning, Mr Burns. I'm Justine Ryan, your new probationary head chef,' she said past a brilliant but much-forced smile. 'Your month's trial sounds like an excellent idea, and I'm quite prepared to accept those terms if you are.'

She reached out, stretching her arm across the vast expanse of desk-top and fighting against the desire to close her eyes. What if he ignored her, refused to shake hands? Or, worse yet, threw her bodily out of his restaurant?

She didn't bother to try and hide her sigh of relief as his black, beetling brows lifted first in surprise, then in accompaniment to a broad smile as he rose and took her fingers gently in his own.

'I'm delighted to meet you again so soon, Miss Ryan,' he said smoothly. 'It's rather a pleasure to meet someone who can quickly grasp the essence of a situation and respond accordingly.' Without freeing her fingers, he slipped round the corner of the desk and led her graciously towards the plush sofa. 'Please, sit down and I'll get us a drink. Then we can discuss the job and all that's involved.'

Justine sank into the plush luxury, her knees suddenly weak. 'Brandy and lemonade for me, thanks,' she replied to a querying eyebrow as he reached the drinks cabinet.

A moment later he placed the drink in her hand, ignoring the tremble in fingers that took it gingerly from him with every expectation of dropping the heavy glass. 'Now, Justine, let me say first that I'm very impressed by your resumé and references. Your application is one of the best I've seen in years, bar the typing of course.' And he grinned mischievously at her. 'What made you decide to leave your last position and seek a job here at Wyatt's?'

Justine found his grin had relaxed her, at least enough to reply after she'd gained yet another moment's grace by slowly sipping at the cold drink. 'It was time to leave,' she said carefully. 'I'd learned all I could, and since I reckoned myself ready to take on a head chef's job, your position came up at just the right time. I ... especially liked the relative isolation. I'm not much of a city girl at heart, I suppose. It was ... just time to leave the nest, that's all.'

'That's ... all?' He leaned back against the plump cushions of the settee, his expression expecting, demanding more detail.

Suddenly wary, Justine threw him a quick glance and then concentrated her expression on a huge painting which dominated the opposite wall. Not for anything would she reveal the true reasons for her departure, the conversation innocently overheard that had blasted her out of the complacency created by her comfortable job as assistant head chef at a smart Sydney restaurant.

She had been checking stores in the establishment's enormous pantry when she had quite innocently found herself the unseen listener to a conversation between her volatile French employer and one of the city's most influential restaurant columnists.

It was at first complimentary to hear her talents described as excellent, but what followed was less complimentary by far.

'Of course she is only a woman,' her employer had said with typical Gallic chauvinism. 'Perhaps she has even the dedication to become a chef *magnifique*, but it is not likely. Still, she is ... decorative.'

The columnist had laughed his acceptance of that remark, adding one of his own to the effect that he would far prefer Justine in the bedroom than the kitchen.

'I also,' said her employer. 'And perhaps that too will eventuate before too long. She has remarkably little confidence in herself, perhaps because she is so ... tall. *Mon Dieu!* Those legs! All the way up to here! Ah yes, soon I think I must evaluate her ... other talents. She will be compliant; she too much likes her job here to be otherwise.'

It had been all Justine could do to keep from confronting the men right then and there, but she held her temper until they had passed beyond earshot. She slipped out of the pantry then, her face flushed with restrained rage, and later that evening had allowed her temper full rein only in the safety of her own flat.

'Swine!' she had muttered over and over, visualising all sorts of appropriate revenge upon the bustling, tubby little Frenchman. She'd steamed and raged at the nerve of the man, but was honest enough to realise that his assessment of her wasn't totally unjustified. She did enjoy—had enjoyed—her work at the restaurant. Too much so, obviously.

Throughout her training and the long string of jobs that followed, she had done everything possible to play down her admitted sexuality. Being five foot ten, with a more than excellent figure and wholesome blonde prettiness, she had often been required to exercise firm dealing with men both on and off the job. As a result she had become quite adept at handling the opposite sex.

Indeed, she had no doubts about handling her employer when the time came, but after nearly a year without so much as a pass from him, the comments he had made that day indicated a remarkable patience. She was forced to doubt seriously that she could keep him at bay and hang on to the job at the same time, and frankly she wasn't inclined to bother.

At breakfast the next morning she studiously went through the papers, and the Wyatt's advertisement leapt out at her with the clarity of a dream come true. She had immediately replied to it, and had found no hesitation leaving her former job when Wyatt Burns had replied favourably to her application.

But now? Faced with a decidedly arrogant man who hadn't wanted a woman chef in the first place, did she dare admit that she had left her former position because of man troubles? Not likely!

'Yes,' she replied without hesitation, 'that's all.'

One eyebrow raised slightly and his eyes surveyed her face with unrestrained pleasure. 'And what about your boy-friend ... or whatever? Won't being this far from the centre of things cause you any personal problems?'

'Not that I can imagine,' she retorted, reluctant to admit that there wasn't any boy-friend or whatever, indeed there never had been anyone who mattered to her more than her work and an inordinate requirement for personal privacy that she seemed to have inherited from her father, now dead. Despite a wealth of experience in the working world, Justine had yet to meet the man who could stir her inner self to anything beyond the most casual interest.

'Hmm,' he murmured, then shifted the tone of the conversation. 'And what do you know about Wyatt's, apart from what was in the advertisement?'

'Not a great deal,' she replied honestly. 'Although I do know the house is noted for the very best of old-fashioned English cooking, the sort John Bull always wanted but seldom got. And that you've a reputation as a rather exacting but fair employer.'

He grinned wickedly. 'Despite being a chauvinist who wouldn't have a woman chef? Perhaps we'd better discuss that and see if it helps to clear the air.'

Justine's face darkened; they'd been getting along so well and now he had to go and spoil it, she thought. But before she could reply he had already begun.

'The basic reason,' he said with firm authority in his

voice, 'is not chauvinism—it's accommodation.'

Justine looked at him with obvious bewilderment on her face. What was he talking about? She became wary again, sensing a trap of some kind.

'True! Most of the employees here live on the premises; I'll show you the set-up later. I'm actually quite proud of it, since it set a milestone in employer–employee relations when I started it, and most of my people have been more than happy with the situation. But—and here I admit to some prejudice, at least—the design never considered the possibility that the head chef might be female, never mind female, young and extremely attractive. Another drink?'

Justine hesitated, then decided that as he was having one, she might as well join him. But only one, she decided; her head felt a bit light from the last one.

He poured the drinks and returned to seat himself beside her, lifting his glass in a silent toast before continuing. 'Now that I think about it,' he said, 'I think I'll retract that bit about prejudice. There's a series of flats for the more significant staff, you see, including the assistant head chef, the two head waiters and our hostess, or maitresse d'hôtel, if you prefer that term. They're all in a special block which I'll show you later, and if there was a spare flat going there, we wouldn't have the problem we have.'

'I do think you're beating around the bush,' Justine said at that point, her curiosity aroused and slowly being churned to fresh anger by his shilly-shallying. 'What problem exactly?'

He grinned wickedly, devilish lights swimming into his dark eyes. 'The problem of you and me sharing this house,' he chuckled. 'You see, the head chef's apartment is right next to mine, on the top floor.'

To say she was taken aback would definitely be an understatement. Justine felt as if somebody had yanked the rug from under her feet.

'I ... see,' she faltered. And then, more strongly,

'But what kind of problem is that? Unless of course you're suggesting . . .'

'Don't be ridiculous!' he snapped. 'And I don't sleepwalk either, for your information.'

'I certainly wasn't suggesting any such thing,' Justine retorted. 'I simply, honestly, don't see the problem—that's all. This is the twentieth century, after all, and you did say, or at least imply, separate apartments. So what's the problem—do you expect me to infringe on your privacy or what?'

'Not at all,' he replied calmly, no longer showing any trace of anger. 'I would simply prefer to avoid any undue . . . talk. Or . . . complications.'

'What kind of complications?' Justine felt her anger building up again. What did he expect, that she'd be kicking down his bedroom door in a bid to compromise him?

'Not from you,' he assured her. 'It's just that—well, on occasion we find it necessary to . . . shall we say sleep over the occasional guest who drinks too much and doesn't dare risk the highway, and I simply wouldn't want any of them getting the wrong idea about your presence in the guest wing.'

'I think I can look after myself,' Justine replied with what she hoped was a suitably scornful look. 'The door to my flat will have a lock, I presume? I can assure you that I've managed to keep my reputation quite intact so far, and I can't imagine having serious problems in an establishment of this quality.'

'Thank you,' he replied drily. 'And I must admit, now that I recall your previous employer's reputation, if you could keep him in line you shouldn't have much trouble with any of our guests.'

'Well, thank *you*,' Justine retorted. 'And now that we've got that straightened out, perhaps you'd like to show me this infamous apartment. Or have you changed your mind about the whole thing?'

'Certainly not! If anything I'm becoming less apprehensive,' he replied. 'Despite a rather prickly temper, you seem to be as professional in your attitudes as I'd have expected. More so, in fact. If your cooking is of the same standard, which I fully expect it will be, you'll go along swimmingly here.'

'I certainly hope so,' Justine replied, her anger deflated by his candour.

'Good,' he said, rising to his feet. 'Now I suggest we do a little cook's tour, if you'll pardon the pun, and then you can see about getting yourself settled before we put your talents to the test.'

'But ... but how can you try me out today?' Justine asked wonderingly. 'I mean, aren't you closed today?'

'Wyatt's is certainly closed today, but Wyatt's stomach doesn't follow orders quite so easily,' he replied. 'And since somebody has to cook me lunch, it might as well be you ... or does the idea frighten you?'

'No ... of course not,' said Justine, lying only a little. 'But I haven't ... I mean ... well, I haven't even *seen* the kitchen yet. I don't know what's on hand, or ... or anything. And it's practically noon now.'

'All the better to test you with,' he replied with a malicious grin. 'Now come and have a quick look around.'

The restaurant, Justine found during their quick tour, was actually four facilities in one, and the house was also divided into two quite different decors. One side was quite traditionally Olde English, with its own pub style bar which featured low beams, plenty of dark wood and imposing bay windows. She liked it immediately.

The private dining room which accompanied the bar was, in Wyatt Burns' words, 'really for those of our guests who pretend to the nobility—or at least have denied their convict ancestry for so long they now believe their own lies.'

Justine looked quickly up at him then, expecting a

look of wry cynicism. But he was only stating facts as he saw them, or so it appeared.

The room was exquisitely decorated, with heavy, well-kept period furniture and furnishings that gave an immediate feeling of comfort and quality. The same applied, to a lesser degree, in the larger common room which served as a second dining room.

When Wyatt Burns led the way through the archway in which he had first appeared to her, Justine's lip curled in a hidden smile as she remembered the rather explosive introduction. She only just managed to compose herself as they crossed the hallway to the other side of the restaurant, where a much more modern decor prevailed. Here, gleaming chrome and the now-familiar blue-on-blue colour scheme provided a style and contemporary luxuriousness for which no expense had been spared.

'The staff calls this side of the house Swinging London,' Wyatt Burns told her with a faint smile. A jerk of his head returned her attention to the portion they had already seen as he added, 'That part's known as The Manor House.'

Justine couldn't have held back the giggle that burbled up through her long throat. 'That's just beautiful,' she chortled. 'I'm glad somebody around here has a sense of humour.'

Her chuckle died in mid-stream as she caught his eye and suddenly realised she had just implied that he had no such sense of humour. The look he gave her was positively scathing.

She refrained, then, from commenting that she much preferred the older, more traditional styling of The Manor House, which to her eyes held a warmth and charm that was quite lacking in the more modern sections of the establishment. When he led her through the second bar, complete with chrome and glass, mirrors, midnight blue leather and revolving chandeliers, she contented herself with a muted 'Very interesting' and didn't say anything further.

But when they reached the kitchens, an immaculate area of modern appliances, spotless cleanliness and thoroughly planned work spaces, she didn't bother to try and conceal her true feelings.

'My goodness! It's absolutely heavenly,' she sighed. The polished stainless steel gave back reflections of Dutch blue tiles, warm wooden chopping blocks and copper-bottomed pots and pans. A chef's delight, no question about it.

Justine forgot about Wyatt Burns, forgot entirely her initial hassles and strong feelings towards his chauvinistic attitude. Like a dancer, she spun happily through the kitchen, touching everything, seeing everything in a haze of cheery delight. Already her mind was alight with ideas; she could hardly wait to start working her own influence into the place that was now her domain.

'It's exquisite!' she cried, swirling around to face a pair of dark eyes that watched her as if she were a child at a candy-shop counter. She didn't care! This kitchen cried out for appreciation, for the touch of someone who could appreciate not only its functional nature, but its inherent warmth and comfort as well.

Silently, Wyatt Burns steered her towards the huge walk-in pantries, where condiments and assorted staples were neatly, properly stacked and arranged, then to the enormous cold room where two large freezers took up respective corners and a mighty butcher's block dominated the central portion. They didn't, thank goodness, stay long in the cold room; just enough so that Justine could gain a quick impression of the layout.

The pantries were a different matter. She poked and probed through them item by item, totally oblivious to the possible boredom of her tall companion as she mentally composed lists of what was there and what wasn't, what she'd want to order now, this very minute, for *her* kitchen.

'I – presume you approve?' The question emerged

in a dry, hardly encouraging tone, but Justine was so vividly impressed at the kitchen facilities she hardly noticed.

'It's magnificent! Absolutely tremendous,' she cried, turning to find herself almost in Wyatt Burns' arms, he was so close behind her.

Strong, lean fingers reached out to grasp her upper arms and keep her from tumbling even closer, and for just an instant she saw . . . gentleness? It couldn't have been . . . in dark eyes that seemed to reach out and grasp at her.

The touch of his fingers burned through the light fabric of her suit, sending tingling sensations far beyond the point of contact. She was all too conscious, then, of the strong, firm mouth only inches from her own, of the heady, masculine scent of his aftershave, the stern, smooth jawline and muscular column of throat.

'I'm glad,' he growled, releasing her so abruptly she almost fell. 'Come and have a peep at your flat, and then you can set about putting your talents on display by making us lunch.'

Wyatt turned on his heel and stalked away, leaving Justine to follow, and she was thankful at least for that. It was much easier to regain her composure behind his back than while facing those dark, fathomless eyes.

A separate staircase led to a broad, carpeted hall on the third floor of the massive house, and Wyatt Burns stepped along quickly with scant regard for the girl trying to follow him in suddenly-clumsy high-heeled shoes.

Stopping in front of a heavy, ornately-carved door, he drew a massive key from his pocket and fitted it to the cunningly disguised lock, twisting open the fitting with one flick of his wrist and then handing the key to Justine.

'I think perhaps I should warn you,' he said softly, 'this is the only suite in the place that we've never

altered from its original form. You may find it . . . unusual, at first, but I assure you it's quite comfortable.'

'I'm sure it will be,' Justine replied, not overly concerned by his warning. During her early years in the
restaurant trade, especially while training in Paris, she
had found herself living in some rather outlandish surroundings. She couldn't imagine any apartment in this
stylish mansion being worse than some she had encountered.

'Right—in you go for a look around; I'll just nip
down and fetch up your bags from the car, if that's all
right,' he said, and took her nod of assent without
further comment.

Justine held the huge key in one hand as she flung
open the heavy door and stepped inside, only to drop
the key from nerveless fingers at her first sight of the
interior.

At first glance it was . . . incredible! Plush draperies
flowed over wide casement windows, matched by
period furniture that showed every evidence of loving
care. A small settee and matching chairs, a tidy little
tea table, and in one corner a small kitchenette. Across
from her, a wide archway revealed an enormous four-
poster bed, complete with canopy and fringes. And on
the walls—on virtually every wall—mirrors.

Walking as if on eggshells, Justine tiptoed through
the sleeping area to peep into a large, well-appointed
but old-fashioned bathroom. More mirrors, but
equally interesting, a bidet.

Turning back to the bedroom, she gingerly lowered
herself on to the side of the four-poster, looked around
her, and gasped with suspicion. It was confirmed when
she lay back for an instant against the pillows and let
her eyes search the room.

'I don't believe this,' she whispered. 'It just . . . can't
be!'

Then a whisper of noise from the hallway brought
her off the bed in a flurry of nylon tights against a

silken coverlet, and when Wyatt Burns stepped into the room with her two cases in his hands, she was on her feet and facing him.

'Well, what do you reckon?' he asked, not bothering to hide the mocking laughter in his eyes.

Justine held her temper, allowing the words to emerge under full control. 'Do you mean to tell me,' she asked, 'that all of your head chefs—all men—have actually *lived* in this . . . this suite?'

'Well, they slept here,' he replied, setting her bags down carefully. 'But then I suspect none of them was quite as astute as you, Miss Ryan.'

'Astute?' Justine laughed bitterly. 'But it's obvious to anyone, surely. This . . . this is a . . . a . . .'

'A very nice suite? I agree entirely.' His grin was totally wicked now, deliberately taunting.

CHAPTER TWO

'It's a *brothel*!'

Justine's voice slipped an octave as she spat out the accusation.

'Really? Why, Miss Ryan, I wouldn't have thought your ... experience was of a type to provide such instant recognition,' Wyatt replied.

'Don't be obscene!' she snapped.

'I'm not being obscene, and this is *not* a brothel,' he replied calmly. 'Although it was, I must admit. Indeed, the whole place was ... once. One of the most posh such establishments in all of New South Wales, if my memory of history serves me. Also a sly grog shop.'

'I don't care what it was,' Justine retorted. 'It's what it *is* that concerns me.'

'It is ... whatever you choose to make it,' he replied. 'And in keeping with the reputation—the current reputation—of the house, I certainly would not expect you to take your surroundings to heart. Besides, you're not the type.'

'Well, thank you *so* much,' she replied, eyes flashing green with rage. 'I suppose you think that was some kind of compliment.'

'Merely a statement of the obvious,' he said grimly. 'Now if you'll tell me where to put these cases, I'll leave you to freshen up before you start on our lunch.'

'You can put them back in the car,' Justine snapped.

'My word! That was the shortest month in history,' he drawled. 'Still, suit yourself.'

'I ... I didn't say I wouldn't take the job,' Justine

stammered, suddenly unsure of herself. 'Merely that I wouldn't stay here in this ... this ...'

'Brothel. I heard you the first time,' he said. 'But where would you live, then? I can't have my head chef sleeping out in her car in the parking lot, and I'm afraid my own suite would be a bit crowded with both of us ...'

'Stop it! Just stop it!' she cried. 'You're going out of your way just to ... to tease and humiliate me.'

'I'm doing no such thing,' he snapped back, anger making his dark eyes darker. Striding forward, grabbing her by the wrist as he passed, he pulled Justine with him to the small kitchenette area and started flinging open doors.

'Look at this!' Cunningly concealed in the period furnishings were each and every modern gadget and convenience she could have asked for, even to a small microwave oven. Fully exposed, it was perhaps the most perfect little kitchenette Justine had ever seen.

'And this!' Doors and drawers were opened in the heavy wall units to reveal a colour television, an expensive stereo system, even a collection of records.

'And—finally—this!' he stormed, slamming the entry door and reaching out to shoot home a set of concealed draw bolts. Then he flipped one finger to show her the tiny spy window in the door itself.

'Every possible convenience, Miss Ryan. Even to a security system. I don't apologise for what this suite was, nor shall I, but by God, if you can't manage to make a home for yourselves despite the rather colourful historical overtones, then I can only suggest you've got too much imagination for your own good.'

He released her wrist and stared down at her with eyes like black, river-washed pebbles. 'So there it is—first and last chance all in one go. I am going to my office, now. Either come along and say goodbye, or come and collect me for our lunch at two o'clock.'

Before Justine could manage any sort of reply, he had re-opened the heavy door and slipped through it, closing it with delicate positiveness behind him.

'Well!' she gasped out loud—and then looked around her, wide-eyed in a dozen mirrored reflections. No matter where she looked, she was confronted by the figure of a tall, slim young woman with a crown of blonde hair and lips that trembled from the ferocity of the encounter.

Suddenly the humour of it all struck her and she turned to flash a wink that was returned tenfold. Then she laughed aloud, almost expecting to hear echoes from her host of reflections. But only her own voice made its muted way around the lush carpeting and furnishings.

Flinging herself full-length on the bed, she lifted her legs and bicycled, like a child at play, laughing almost hysterically now at the reflected images of herself.

Without Wyatt Burns' stern-visaged image in the mirrors, they lost a great deal of their intimidation. And, Justine realised with startling clarity, their suggestiveness. Was it indeed his presence, rather than the mirrors themselves, that lent the aura of sensuality to the room?

'Can't think of that or I *will* be sleeping in the car,' she muttered, hefting one suitcase up on to the bureau so that she could rummage out some kind of apron and get on with her lunch preparations. It seemed no longer under question—she had the job and she'd stay, at least for the trial month.

En route to the kitchen, she ducked out and retrieved a third case from the trunk of her car, this one a solidly-made wooden case containing her personal knives and an omelette pan and sauce pan, utensils she had lovingly nurtured and cared for since her student days.

Back in the kitchen, she stood for a moment, professionally assessing the spotless work areas and their correlation to the storage, chilling and cooking arrangements. After several minutes she gave a satisfied nod and a silent accolade to whoever had designed the kitchens. Wyatt Burns? Possible, she decided. At the very least the best expert he could hire; Wyatt Burns didn't strike her as a man to accept second best and he certainly hadn't stinted in providing for his chef.

'Which means I'd better not try to cut corners, either,' she mused, picking up a leather-bound menu and seating herself at what was obviously the chef's office desk, tucked into a handy alcove next to the cool room.

The menu ran the gamut of traditional English dishes from unusual soups such as Cheshire and Ballymoney oyster, to more readily recognisable ones such as Cock-a-Leekie and Brown Windsor. Roast beef and Yorkshire pudding vied for attention with baked ham, Lancashire hotpot and squab pie. Justine heaved a small sigh of relief when she realised that most of the dishes were just explanations on the menu. The basic list, according to a notice near the end of the menu, was exactly that—basic. The bulk of the menu was determined by the availability of ingredients and the seasonal varieties.

Rising, menu in hand, she moved over to peer into the vegetable storage, swiftly correlating what she saw with what might be expected from the menu.

Unsure what Wyatt Burns might really expect for lunch, a hearty meal or merely a stopgap until dinner time, she chose a middle path. Three courses would surely be enough, she thought, having spied several fresh trout in the huge refrigerator. Here was her main course, wrapped in bacon as the menu suggested. Now for dessert. Turning directly to the menu, she ran a steady finger down the list as she thought about the ingredients she'd noticed. Boodle's orange fool—per-

fect. A quick and easy dessert, using the handy quick-
chill section of the refrigerator and the two fresh
sponge cakes on hand.

Concentrating on those two courses first, Justine
worked swiftly, thankful she'd been able to find
the overall style apron that would protect her
suit.

As she assembled the ingredients and implements,
she was forced by her time factor to dispense with her
usual habit of cleaning up as she went. That would
simply have to wait. Once the fool was chilling and the
trout ready to be popped into the oven, she turned her
attention to some kind of starter course with less time
in hand than she would have liked.

There was a tureen of soup, but she rejected it. That
belonged, she presumed, to her predecessor; this lunch
would be exclusively hers. Then she remembered a
bucket of superb fresh mushrooms she'd noticed
tucked in a corner of the cold room, and her spirits
lifted. The starter she had in mind wasn't on Wyatt
Burns' menu, but it was in keeping with the tone of
his restaurant, and most important it was quick, easy
and attractive.

Unwelcome thoughts were forced away as she concentrated on the required chopping and cutting and
stirring. Just in time, she had everything ready, and
she tossed off the apron, set out the first course on a
tray, and shouldered her way through the swinging
doors into the restaurant areas.

Swinging around, a pleased and happy grin on her
lips, she found her way blocked by a tall, almost forbidding figure that was so unexpected she almost
dropped the tray.

Long fingers reached out to steady it—and her. 'I've
put us in the Manor House private dining room,'
Wyatt said with a slow grin. 'I'll take this; you trot
ahead and check that I've set everything out
properly.'

Justine obeyed silently, smiling her pleasure as she entered the narrow archway to find a table laid with a pale blue cloth, the navy-and-white china and gleaming silver providing a complementary touch. She ran a critical eye over the place settings, finding one spoon too many and deftly removing the offending items just as Wyatt arrived.

'Please sit down,' she said as he gallantly held back her chair after carefully placing the tray on one corner of the table. She carefully served the mushrooms in a circle on each plate, artistically arranging the dish for maximum visual effect.

Wyatt seated her, then reached out to pluck a bottle of chilled vintage Riesling from its leather-covered cooler. 'I didn't know exactly what you'd planned, but I think this will go well with just about anything,' he smiled, and at her nod of agreement he poured each of them a glass.

Justine waited until Wyatt had begun to eat before starting herself, and as she chewed unconsciously, her entire attention locked on his face, seeking a reaction to the dish.

But he said nothing, or at least nothing about the meal. Instead, he carried on a witty and urbane conversation that quickly drew in Justine's opinions and gradually relaxed her. After his initial assistance, he made no attempt to help, but let her carry away the used dishes and return with fresh ones. He did, of course, rise each time to seat her, but from a man of his experience she would have expected no less.

It was comforting, at least, to see him thoroughly clean up his plate, even to using the remains of a bread roll to finish up the tiniest morsels of mushroom sauce. He quite obviously enjoyed the trout, too, she thought, but she wasn't all that certain of his reaction to the fool.

When the meal was finally ended, she brought their coffee and liqueurs to the ornate coffee table sitting in front of a sofa that filled one bay window. When Wyatt offered her a cigarette, she reached out gratefully.

Justine didn't often smoke, but her resolution had never been intended to cover situations like this. Not since the first meal she had prepared for her first tutor in Paris had she felt so totally unsure of herself, doubting what her own taste-buds had already confirmed was an excellent meal.

She dragged slowly at the cigarette, however, knowing she wasn't honestly enjoying it, and she stubbed it out half-smoked, eventually. She took a sip of her coffee, found it tasteless, and was surprised to find the excellent port equally so. Damn it, she thought, why doesn't he say something?

Finally she could take no more, and despite the realisation that he'd provoked her, she clicked her coffee cup down in its saucer and turned to glare directly at the tall figure that lounged against one corner of the sofa with a liqueur glass dangling insolently from his agile fingers.

'Well?' she demanded.

'Well ... what?' he drawled, eyes trailing lazily across her face and his lips registering deliberate misunderstanding.

Justine flushed. He was going to make it deliberately difficult for her, but she had no choice but to continue. 'What did you think?' she asked.

He shrugged, broad shoulders rippling the fine cut of his dark suit jacket. 'You know what thought did?' he replied, eyes laughing at her.

'What does that have to do with anything?' she countered warily. She did *not* know what thought did, having grown up so long with the question but never having heard anybody even attempt to answer it. Surely, she thought, there *was* no answer. It was merely one of those parental lines used to manipulate children's excuses. How often had she excused a silly action by saying 'But I thought . . .' only to have that same question thrown at her?

'You don't know, do you?'

She didn't reply immediately, but after a second was forced into the admission. Her racing mind created no answers, only a kaleidoscope of confused colours.

'No, I don't.'

His eyes screamed out mocking laughter. 'I suppose what you really wanted was my opinion of the meal?' he said then.

'Brilliant deduction,' she snapped, temper frayed by the mental aspects of her ordeal as much as by his careless, laughing attitude.

'Yes, I'm quite good that way,' he agreed. 'You, however, need a few lessons.'

'Lessons?' It came out as a squeak, so shaken was she by the comment.

'In self-confidence, not cooking,' he replied with a flash of scowl. 'Good heavens, Justine . . . you sat there and ate the same things I did, but you're so nervous I'll bet you never even tasted them!'

This time she couldn't answer, though she realised her downcast glance was reply enough.

'Oh, all right,' he said. 'Your cooking, Miss Ryan, is indisputably excellent. The garnishes were perfect and the main course and dessert were exactly to menu standard, although you did something extra to the trout that I can't place.'

Justine heaved a sigh of relief, quite unconsciously. The gust of breath made the tall man beside her grin fleetingly before he continued.

'However, I noticed the starter course was something that's not from our usual menu,' he said. 'I have to ask if it's a traditional-type dish, because I'd like very much to have you add it to the menu if it would be appropriate.'

Justine could afford to relax now. 'It's an old family recipe,' she said. 'And yes, it would fit, since my mother claimed it went back to the mid-1800s. It comes from around London in what people have referred to as the garden counties, but I don't know the proper name. Mom always just called it Mushrooms in a Circle.'

'That's a quaint name,' he mused, strong brow furrowing ever so slightly. 'But what's in it, really?'

Justine shrugged. 'Well, mostly mushrooms, of c ...' She halted abruptly, her words throttled by the thunderous look of her companion's face. 'Wh-what ... what's the matter?' she finally blurted.

The words emerged individually, only three of them and each carrying its own placard of horror and revulsion. 'I ... hate ... mushrooms!' Wyatt's face was a study in barely-controlled fury and his voice a muted maelstrom that threatened Justine, the room and everything else around them.

The first thing that flashed into her mind, unbidden but vivid in memory, was the sight of Wyatt cleaning every single morsel of that starter course from his own plate and then leering suggestively, hungrily, at the bit Justine herself hadn't eaten. She couldn't help it; her lower lip trembled, quivered, then erupted with the bolt of laughter that shot from within her.

Even as the laughter brought tears to her face and stopped her from any form of apology, she saw his face blacken with increased anger. And the angrier he became, the more she had to laugh, her sense of humour stronger even, it seemed, than her sense of self-preservation.

Finally she managed a modicum of control, leaning back against the arm of the sofa with her bosom still heaving and tears streaming down her cheeks. Wyatt, by this time, had reverted to an icy, fragile control. He looked ready to draw and quarter her.

'I didn't think it was at all that humorous,' he growled through snarling teeth.

Nothing could have been more calculated to rekindle

the laughter that lurked just beneath the surface of Justine's barely calm exterior. It bubbled forth again, cluttering the words as she chuckled, 'Yes . . . but then you . . . you don't like . . . mushrooms, either . . . except when you're eating them.'

And she broke up again, this time with every inner fibre striving vainly for control. Part of her mind screamed at her to stop laughing her way out of her job, but another simply gave in to the ridiculousness of it all.

Wyatt, a rigid, fiery figure that fairly radiated murderous rage, sat staring at her through eyes like wet coal until finally his will linked with hers and once again the laughter was subdued.

'I do think,' he said then, 'that you go out of your way to provoke me, Miss Ryan.'

Miss Ryan it was now; but only a moment before she'd been Justine and the swine had liked her mushrooms, deny it or no. Temper swept in to scourge the laughter, and her eyes blazed green.

'In a pig's eye!' she snapped. 'It strikes me, Mr Wyatt Burns, that you don't know what in the hell you like, and if that's the kind of blind ignorance you use in running your restaurant, then heaven help your customers! I'm surprised you don't feed them on fish and chips. You ate your mushrooms, and liked them. You even coveted mine, damn you. And then you have the audacity to shout at me. Oh . . . oh . . .!'

She halted then, sure she'd already overstepped herself but nonetheless afraid she'd say something really awful if she continued.

Wyatt had no such compunctions. 'Go on,' he said in a voice like death. 'Your next line should include something about my lack of a sense of humour, or is that after the next outburst of hysterical laughter?'

It was like a cold glass of water in the face. Justine shivered visibly, making no attempt to hide it. Fear closed her mouth, but it couldn't stop her lips from trembling as he reached out to grasp her wrist, pulling her towards him in a single, inexorable motion.

His black eyes bored into hers as she fetched up in the circle of his arm, her breasts crushed against his chest as he lowered his mouth to hers in a kiss that cruelly ravaged the softness of her mouth. Her lips parted, unable to withstand the onslaught of his mouth, and her head was thrown back to expose her throat to fingers that traced a design of passion and sheer masculine domination along the taut tendons there.

She couldn't breathe; she couldn't think; she couldn't move. Yet all her senses came alight as if he'd attacked her with a blowtorch of passion. She could feel his heart thudding against her breasts, smell the clean, tangy scent of him, hear the raging of his own breath as he kissed her, ravished her with his mouth, with his entire being.

Never in all her life had Justine experienced such an assault. Wyatt's obvious experience and the barely-controlled anger which had obviously prompted his ravishment made him invincible. She didn't, couldn't fight him; her body and mind could only accept his domination.

Then, as suddenly as it had begun, it was ended. He straightened her up into a sitting position with a gentleness that belied his earlier passion, and when he spoke his voice was totally controlled.

'And how is that for a sense of humour, dear Justine?' he said very softly, no longer touching her, but his eyes continued the assault, roving with careless abandonment over the curves of her body, the flushed trembling of her lips.

Justine fought for breath, for control of her shattered emotions. She simply could not believe that her body could feel so suddenly . . . cold, bereft of the close heat of Wyatt's chest against her. Her eyes were no longer green, but a muted, in-between colour that revealed the confusion inside her.

Until finally she met his eyes and saw the raw mockery that flashed towards her like lightning bolts. He was laughing at her, nothing more. Even the savagery of his assault had been no more than an act, she thought. With that realisation came a strange calm, a passive control that allowed her mind to work, her lips to move.

'Personally,' she said scornfully, 'I much preferred the mushrooms.'

'Personally,' he replied with an infuriating and quite unnerving calm, 'I much preferred you! Although,' and a secretive smile flickered at the side of his mouth, 'I think I could develop a taste for mushrooms, as well.'

'I think that might be safer,' a voice from within Justine replied without her consciously helping. 'Even though some mushrooms are poisonous.'

'*All* women are,' he retorted without so much as raising his voice. And then, totally unexpectedly, he held out his hand to her and grinned broadly. 'You'll take over as Number One chef in the morning, then. I think we'll go well together.'

Justine was struck dumb. Her every thought, from slapping his face to simply walking out and leaving the dirty dishes behind her, disappeared in a puff of nothingness.

'I . . . mm . . . yes . . . *yes!*' she replied finally, her hand already caught in the muscular grasp of his fingers as he shook her hand.

'Right! I'll have somebody rounded up to clean up after that most delightful lunch, and if you'll be ready at six I'll return the compliment by taking you somewhere for a dinner you don't have to even think about cooking,' he said, and had left her before she could reply.

Justine leaned back into the softness of the cushions behind her, her head swimming with confusion that wasn't at all helped by her unconsciously sipping at the remains of her port. Suddenly it all seemed like a dream. Surely she couldn't have—in one single morning—been given a new job, a former brothel to live in, and been kissed so very, very thoroughly?

Without Wyatt's unnerving presence, she was gradually more able to evaluate what had happened, and after a moment she found herself even more incredulous than before. The incident concerning the mushrooms took on new implications with hindsight; he must have been having her on. Nobody, and surely nobody so deeply involved in restaurant management, she thought, could possibly have eaten that dish without knowing what it contained.

But then what had he been doing? Testing her, in some way, but for what purpose? Did he expect to find her reaction when a dissatisfied customer demanded her presence? Or had he been playing some much more devious game of his own?

For one ludicrous instant Justine found herself wondering if it had all been a carefully constructed scenario building up to the unexpected kiss. Then she laughed aloud at the sheer ridiculousness of that idea. Wyatt Burns surely needed no such artificial organisation to provide him with the opportunity to kiss her, or any other woman. It was quite obviously an area in which he had a wealth of experience.

'A wealth of experience indeed,' she mused half aloud, then reached up with one index finger to stroke at her soft, still tender lips.

'The nerve of the man!' she muttered, knowing she should very definitely be angry but not overly surprised that she was not. After all, he'd only kissed her, Justine thought, only too aware that his simple kiss had held more sexual overtones than the most blatant approach she had ever received from any other man—even in Paris.

Or had that, too, been only an act? Justine racked

her brain over that particular question, unable to find
even a hint of an answer because something kept insisting that his professed aversion to mushrooms
wasn't an act. He'd seemed genuinely angry then,
even if it didn't make sense to her.

'Not that I should be complaining, I suppose,' she
muttered ruefully. 'Here I am, agreed to having dinner
with him, and any fool could see that it's entirely the
opposite of what I should be doing.'

For just an instant she thought of changing her mind
and refusing. Certainly his unprovoked assault gave
her all the justification she could ask for? But it was a
fleeting thought; she knew in her heart that she
wouldn't change her mind. What she would do, however, was ensure that the evening provided no opportunity for a repeat performance of that afternoon's
kiss. There was something . . . dangerous in allowing
too many liberties to a man like Wyatt Burns, Justine
decided.

'Excuse me, ma'am.' The shy, tentative voice interrupted her thoughts, then, and Justine refocused her
eyes to find a tall, slender, dark-haired young girl
standing hesitantly off to one side.

'Yes?' Justine smiled as she replied, not at all sure
the child wouldn't cut and run if she so much as spoke
too loudly. Enormous, doe-like eyes widened at her
response, and the girl seemed to hesitate before speaking.

'Um . . . Mr Wyatt sent me to clean up,' she
blurted.

'I see,' Justine smiled. 'And did he say you should
tell me your name, as well?'

'N-no,' whispered the girl, eyes dropping away as if
she feared Justine would strike her. The girl couldn't
have been much over sixteen, Justine thought, and her
slim young figure was all out of proportion, like that of
a young colt. And the shyness!

'Well, we're hardly going to be able to work together

if I don't know your name,' Justine said gently. 'Mine's Justine.'

'Yes, Miss Ryan. Mr Wyatt told me,' the child replied, then lapsed once again into a watchful silence.

'And do you work here full-time?' Justine asked, carefully ignoring the fact that the girl had yet really to answer the last question. Lord, she thought, if this is any example of my regular kitchen help, I may have made a mistake in staying.

'In . . . in the kitchen,' the girl faltered. 'I . . . I'm hoping to be a chef . . . like you . . . some day.'

'I . . . see,' Justine replied. 'Well then, perhaps we'd best get these dirty dishes back into the kitchen, and perhaps we can talk about it while we're cleaning up, eh?'

'Oh . . . but *I'm* supposed to do the cleaning up,' was the faltering response, and Justine sighed inwardly. She hadn't seen such shyness since . . . since she herself was about fifteen, she realised with wry amusement. And even I could manage to get my name out, she thought. What's wrong with this child?

She slid cautiously to her feet, unable to avoid the oddest idea that one fast move would spook the child into flight. Moving slowly, she gathered up the various dishes and carefully stacked them into the girl's arms.

Then she gathered the rest into her own, mouth quirking in memory of the first time she'd tried to carry too many plates and cups and saucers, and the embarrassing, inevitable result of broken glass and crockery.

'Can you manage all that?' she asked gently. A nod was the only reply, but when she turned to shoulder her way through into the kitchens, the child was right behind her and seemed to be coping well enough.

Justine forced herself to sit down and watch as the girl began the dishwashing, clumsiness transformed to a sort of coltish grace as familiarity reduced the shyness to some extent. She had to restrain the impulse to ask yet again for the girl's name, hoping that it would come without any increased pressure.

It did. Justine almost fell off her stool when the girl looked up from the suds and said, quite unexpectedly, 'My name's Parthenia. Isn't it awful?'

'I don't see why,' Justine replied honestly. 'It's Greek, isn't it? And it means . . . oh, I should know, too . . .'

'It means *sweet virgin*, or at least that's what my father tells me. He's Greek—his name is Sebastian. That's not as awful as Parthenia.' The words poured out, once begun, and Justine was treated to a lengthy account of the girl's history, likes and dislikes, ending with the rather surprising disclosure that Wyatt—along with most of the staff—called Parthenia 'Possum'. Unspoken, but no less obvious, was the fact that Possum thought the sun rose and set in Wyatt Burns.

Which, Justine thought as she went up the stairs to her room a bit later, was hardly to be unexpected. At that age she herself would have been similarly inclined. But not, she vowed fervently, quite so obvious about it. Possum's case of hero-worship was quite the most pronounced she'd ever encountered.

Justine spent the remainder of the afternoon organising her diminutive wardrobe, having a long, refreshing shower and being alternately amused and put off by the multi-faceted images of herself as she moved about the apartment.

'If I were a narcissist, this flat would be perfect,' she mused, stepping from the shower to find herself confronted with views of her body from viewpoints never before available to her. It was mildly disconcerting, she found, and yet . . .

'At least it's very handy to check if my slip is showing,' she said to one image, which giggled back at her silently as she spun herself around to check the flair of the one really good dress she owned. It was supposedly a basic black, the traditional mainstay of any girl's wardrobe, but it was a Parisian basic black, which before the legion of mirrors took on much greater effect than Justine had ever quite realised.

It was cocktail length, with three-quarter sleeves and a high mesh neckline that she had always thought quite decorous, and she looked at it now and realised that the mesh was more provocative than anything else, especially combined with the deep-cut proper neckline and even lower back.

For one panic-stricken moment she thought to change the dress; it would be folly, she thought, to wear something this provocative in light of Wyatt's earlier actions. But Justine realised just as suddenly that she couldn't change it. She simply had nothing else with her that was suitable for anywhere she could imagine Wyatt Burns dining out.

And in any event, there wasn't the time. Even as she rejected the idea and ran a comb through her long, flowing hair, there was a discreet knock at her door.

Grabbing up her handbag and knitted evening stole, she flung open the door to find a resplendent Wyatt leaning with studied casualness against the wall across from it. In his dark evening wear he looked even taller than usual, his eyes somehow more sardonic, his face more devilish above the neat bow tie and gleaming shirt-front.

'Punctual, I see,' he said with a ghost of a grin. 'My, there's just no end to your appeal, Justine.' He slurred out her name, almost but not quite in the French pronunciation, and there was something so personal in the way he said it that Justine felt a warm glow despite his sarcasm.

'So are you . . . punctual, I mean,' she replied, stepping quickly through the doorway and away from the pavilion of mirrors behind her. It was subtle, she thought, but Wyatt didn't miss the gesture.

'Still bugged by the mirrors?' he asked, this time with a distinct grin. 'You're not using your imagination to full advantage, Justine; think what it could do for your love life.'

'The day I need that kind of stimulation, I'll give it away entirely,' she replied tartly. 'If you check your history, you'll find that kind of stimulation was there only for the jaded old men who patronised such places. The . . . girls . . . didn't need such special effects.'

Wyatt laughed, taking her arm as they reached the head of the stairs. 'We must have read different history books, dear child,' he said. 'Although you're half right; for a woman, money is usually a stronger sexual stimulant than mirrors.'

Justine yanked her arm free, almost tripping herself in the process but determined not to be drawn further by his innuendoes. 'For some women, perhaps,' she snapped. 'And if that's the only type you've encountered in your life, then I rather pity you, Mr Burns.'

'The last thing I need is pity . . . from any woman,' he replied calmly enough. But Justine got the feeling her sharp comment had struck home, somewhere in that chauvinistic hide.

Could it be, she wondered, that even the devilish Wyatt Burns had his Achilles heel? Or was she just imagining things, giving way to her own personal preference for men with a bit of gentleness to their nature?

Fortunately, Wyatt chose to alter the tone of the conversation as they reached the bottom of the staircase and stepped out to where he could hand her into the passenger seat of a luxurious automobile.

Speaking as if their earlier fencing hadn't even happened, he leaned above her and asked, 'Have you any objection to Greek food, Justine? If so, please tell me now, while there's time to change our reservation.'

'I have no objection to any type of food, properly done,' she replied honestly enough. During her years of training she'd been exposed to virtually every type of cooking, including the more traditional ethnic dishes common to the restaurant world, and she'd yet to run across any particular style that she didn't enjoy.

'Good,' Wyatt replied, striding round to seat himself behind the wheel. 'Because I think you might find some aspects of the place I've chosen . . . interesting.'

'That would be nice,' Justine replied cautiously and without committing herself too deeply. She refrained from asking if they served mushrooms, though it was on the tip of her tongue.

During the hour-long drive just to the edge of the city, Wyatt contented himself with discussing fairly general topics, mostly concerning his own establishment, its history and the approach he had been developing during the past few years. Justine was a quiet and willing listener, knowing as she did that the more she knew about his attitudes towards the place, the easier her job would be in terms of fitting in.

What she'd seen of Wyatt's thus far had been more than impressive, and his comments during the drive made it even more so.

The restaurant he had chosen wasn't particularly impressive from the outside, but once in the large entryway, Justine was pleasantly surprised to find it fitted out authentically as a proper Greek *taverna*.

And the head waiter who greeted them with effusive buoyancy might well have been Anthony Quinn's understudy for Zorba the Greek. He was absolutely perfect, wild and flamboyant and vivid in the extreme.

He greeted Wyatt like an old friend, which rather surprised Justine. How could a man who claimed to detest ordinary mushrooms cope with the exotic Greek offerings? she wondered.

It was hardly less surprising when Wyatt suggested that *she* choose from the expansive menu, without so much as a word about her avoiding the dreaded mushrooms. 'I hope you know what you're doing,' she cautioned. 'I could get quite carried away.'

'Good. I'm rather hungry,' he replied—and never turned a hair when she chose *tyropita*, then *dolmades* poached in egg-and-lemon sauce, *sofrita*, pork cooked with cabbage, fried squid and finally the delectable *svingi*, honey fritters she remembered from a long-ago trip to Corfu.

They worked their way through the various delicacies in relative silence, and were well into the meal when a brazen outburst of traditional music announced the arrival of the evening's entertainment. Justine looked up in mild curiosity as a scantily-clad dancer vaulted on to the tiny stage, then looked again and promptly dropped her fork in astonishment.

CHAPTER THREE

'I DON'T believe it!' she whispered aloud, but one glance at Wyatt's laughing face told her she'd better believe it. Dancing on the stage with an abandon that went far beyond anything Justine had ever seen in Greece itself was *Possum*!

She couldn't believe her eyes. Shy, wouldn't even tell her name, coltish Parthenia-Possum, *sweet virgin*? Not by any evaluation of her performance before an enthusiastic audience. The music might have been traditionally Greek, along with the food, but Possum's act was deliberately geared to Australian taste, and masculine Australian taste at that, Justine decided.

There was no evidence of shyness, nor of the youthful, unco-ordinated movement she had seen in the kitchen only that afternoon. This Possum was a woman, slender and lightly built to be sure, but no less a woman for all that. There was no mistaking the curve of long, high-kicking legs, nor the wide, flashing smile that promised heaven itself whenever it touched on a male member of the wildly cheering audience.

Especially, Justine noticed almost immediately, on Wyatt Burns himself. She might as well not have existed. Possum's eyes drank in Wyatt's handsome features, her body moved to excite him, her arms moved as if to embrace him. Even from across the room, one couldn't ignore the fire of Possum's deliberate provocativeness.

Nor did he. If anything, Justine decided, his dark eyes flashed encouragement and when the dance was over his hands led the applause with generous enthusiasm.

It was only then that he turned to address Justine with obvious suspicion in his eyes.

'You didn't enjoy it?'

'Oh, I did,' she assured him. 'It's just that . . .'

'. . . that it was a little too flamboyant for your taste? I'm not surprised.'

'That wasn't it at all,' she retorted. 'I was just . . . well . . . surprised, that's all.'

Wyatt stared at her for a long moment, eyes seeming to bore straight through her. Then, suddenly, his eyes widened in understanding and he laughed harshly.

'I think I know what you mean, now,' he said, and abruptly reached out to snare a passing waiter and mutter something at him that Justine didn't catch.

But Wyatt said nothing further to Justine. He merely reached out to refill their wine glasses, his attention quite obviously elsewhere. Only a minute or two elapsed before Justine realised just where, as a swift, slender figure sped across the crowded restaurant towards them.

'Wyatt! Wow! Wasn't that a crowd-pleaser?' Possum cried delightedly as she scooted over to throw her arms around Wyatt's neck.

'It was terrific, Poss,' he replied, making no effort at all to disengage her. 'Almost as good as your act this afternoon, I'd imagine. Which one was it this time?'

To Justine's surprise then, the slender girl winked quite deliberately at her, then transformed before her very eyes.

It was magic! Even in the provocative dancer's gear, Possum instantly became the gauche, shy creature of the kitchen, flighty, skittish, and about fifteen years of age.

Justine could only gape, but Wyatt slapped the girl across the rump in a gesture both familiar and threatening. 'You little witch!' he grinned. 'It's no wonder poor Justine has been watching you as if she couldn't believe her own eyes! I should tell Sebastian to take his belt to you, my girl, not that I reckon it'd do much good.'

Possum, the real Possum—if there was such a person—merely laughed delightedly before switching roles yet again, this time to a harem-girl slave who protested her innocence and pleaded against being beaten. Even Justine had to laugh as Wyatt patiently endured her protestations and then sent the alluring slave off to receive her punishment.

'I'm an ogre, aren't I?' he chuckled when Possum had slipped away through the crowd. 'And I really am sorry, Justine—about this afternoon, I mean. I never thought that little devil would start playing her games with you on first meeting.'

'Don't apologise,' Justine replied. 'What I'd like to know is what she was doing washing dishes in the first place. The girl's a wonderful actress; I've never seen such versatility.'

'You haven't seen Sebastian at his best, either,' he replied. 'The whole family's that way, although it's a toss-up between Possum and Sebastian for top honours.'

'That doesn't answer my question,' she prompted, only to receive a broad smile in reply.

'Not now,' he countered, eyes roving past her to the edge of the stage. 'You're about to see yet another face of our Possum.'

Justine turned to look too, and was by this stage only mildly surprised to see the slender figure ease on to the platform with a guitar in her hands. Seating herself on a high stool, Possum waited until the crowd had quieted of its own volition, then lifted the instrument and began to play and sing what could only have been a love song.

Her voice was light, yet seemed somehow to fill the room, and not a chair shifted, not a voice spoke to break the spell. Even without understanding the words, Justine could feel the haunting mood of the music, and she closed her eyes and let it drift right through her.

A touch on her hand roused her, and she opened her eyes in surprise to find her hand enclosed within Wyatt's, but when she looked over at him, he too was apparently lost in the melody, eyes closed and his muscular body relaxed in his chair.

Justine thought first to remove her hand, then changed her mind abruptly and instead simply closed her own eyes, letting the music take her again. Only now she couldn't let herself drift with it entirely; she was anchored by Wyatt's fingers, all too aware of the warmth of him, the feel of his hand on hers.

She was never sure where the song ended. The music seemed to continue, on and on and on. Then suddenly it wasn't there any more, and her eyes flicked open to find Wyatt's dark eyes soft upon her, studying her face with a gentle expression that disappeared like smoke when his eyes opened.

His voice still held softness, however, though he had to raise it to counter the thunderous applause around them. 'Do you understand Greek?' he asked, then nodded with some mysterious satisfaction when she shook her head.

'Just as well,' he muttered.

'Why? It was a lovely song and the message in it was surely obvious enough.' True, she thought, even though Possum had been singing it directly to Wyatt, while he, in turn, had held Justine's hand throughout most of it. No logic, there.

'I wouldn't have thought you'd have noticed,' he said with a hint of a grin. 'You had your eyes closed practically throughout.'

'I certainly don't see what's wrong with that,' she replied, wondering suddenly why he still held her fingers trapped in his own. She looked down, then, and his eyes followed hers, his fingers releasing her as her mind willed them to.

'If you're ready, perhaps we'd better be going now,'

he said. 'Tomorrow will likely be a long, hard grind for you, so you'll need your beauty sleep.'

Justine couldn't argue, and by the time he'd called for the account and haphazardly signed it, she was ready.

Wyatt drove quickly on the way home, but with great skill and care. He said little, however, until they had left the inner city's crowded streets and were on the main highway south.

'I hope you won't think too badly of Possum,' he said then, bringing the comment up from nowhere. 'It was damned thoughtless of her to have you on this afternoon, and I really do apologise for that, but Possum is . . . unique.'

'She certainly is that,' Justine agreed. 'But I still don't understand what she's doing working as a kitchen hand when she has so many other talents. And you never told me when I asked before, so I suppose you won't now, either.'

'It's simple, really,' he replied, ignoring her jibe entirely. 'Sebastian won't let her. Except in the restaurant, but of course he's very close to being the owner by now, so that sort of keeps it in the family. But to have her on the stage—either acting or singing—no way! I've tried to convince him otherwise, but so far I haven't had much luck.'

'But why won't he let her? I mean, it's such a waste.'

Wyatt shrugged. 'Pure simple chauvinism, to a large degree. Plus the fact, of course, that he'd be much less able to control her if she were on her own, and believe me, Possum is damned hard to control just as she is. To be honest, I can understand his feelings, even agree to some extent, but not totally.'

Justine chuckled. 'Does that mean you're not quite the total chauvinist you appear to be?' she asked provocatively. 'I'd never have believed it.'

His reply was a short bark of laughter followed by a distinctly wolfish grin. 'I'll just bet you wouldn't,' he growled, 'but I'd advise you here and now, dear Justine, not to go making snap judgments. And while you're about it just a gentle warning not to go out of your way to . . . provoke me. I have the feeling there'll be quite enough of that without you specifically working at it.'

'I don't know what you mean,' Justine replied haughtily.

'Of course you don't,' he retorted, voice fairly alive with sarcasm. 'But ignore that for the moment; let's go back to this chauvinism discussion. It's very much a two-edged sword, you know. For instance, when you get married, would you expect to give up your career?'

'I hadn't ever really thought about it,' Justine countered—a blatant lie, but how was he to know?

Wyatt shrugged. 'So think about it now,' he charged. 'It's a fair drive home; you've plenty of time.'

'But it isn't something that particularly affects me,' she hedged, only to have him snort with derision.

'Oh, come now. I don't know why you persist in being obtuse. Of course it affects you. You could meet the right man . . . tomorrow, if you haven't already. What then? Would you accept him insisting that you stay home and be a proper little housewife, abandoning all that training you worked so hard to get?'

'But it just isn't that simple,' she countered. 'I mean, what if he were a farmer, or . . . whatever?'

Wyatt's laugh was deliberately insinuating. 'How many farmers do you expect to meet hiding in my kitchens?' he challenged. 'No, let's be a bit more realistic. What if he were . . . a restaurateur, for instance? Like me?'

Justine shivered . . . visibly, and then prayed he hadn't noticed. How could this man have such an effect on her, she wondered—and in less than a single day?

'I don't think that's at all realistic,' she replied cautiously. 'You're no more looking for a wife than I am for a husband.'

'I warned you about making snap judgments,'

Wyatt said, turning to fix her with his brooding eyes. 'For all you know I've already got one lined up. In fact,' and he flashed his teeth in another wolfish grin, 'maybe I've already got one, full stop.'

'Then that only makes the conversation even more ridiculous,' Justine retorted, heaving a minuscule sigh of relief. Maybe now he'd drop this decidedly uncomfortable discussion. Maybe . . .

They drove nearly a mile in silence before he replied, and the reply was the farthest thing from anything she might have expected.

'You're damned well not going to ask, are you?' he demanded.

'Ask what?' And she wasn't, this time, being deliberately obtuse.

'Whether I've already got a wife, of course. You *were* wondering about it; I could tell by the look in your eye.'

Too close for comfort, that. 'I was doing no such thing,' she lied. 'It's perfectly obvious you haven't got a wife—and if you have she's more to be pitied than censured.'

'Pitied? That'd be the day. And you haven't answered the question.'

'I did so. Besides which, I really couldn't care less one way or the other,' Justine replied.

'Okay.' His reply was calm, but he followed it with a direct switch in tactics. 'Assuming I don't have a wife, and that I was going to marry you, would you expect to keep on working or not?'

'Well, of course I would,' she cried, patience almost at an end. 'What would you expect me to do, stay at home all day and play in my hall of mirrors while you wandered around molesting the hired help?'

Wyatt blithely ignored the anger in her voice, along with her demanded question. 'And what about once the little ones started coming?' he asked. 'I suppose you'd want to be parking them in the vegetable bins so you could keep an eye on them between courses?'

She laughed. The visual images that comment created made it impossible not to laugh. 'Only until they were old enough to help with the washing up,' she giggled.

'I hope your cooking is better than your sense of humour,' Wyatt snapped. 'God! With you and Possum both in the kitchen the place'll be a madhouse!'

'Well, if you want to change your mind about the whole thing, now's the time,' Justine snapped back, unaccountably prickly and sensitive to the slightest nuances in his voice. 'After all, we've each given the other a meal, so that ought to make us square.'

'I don't think you should eat Greek food any more,' he replied without raising his voice. 'It plays hell with your disposition.'

'You don't know anything about my disposition,' Justine replied, her temper visibly frayed.

'And I'm not likely to, since you refuse to give me a straight answer to the simplest of questions,' he countered. 'What's the matter . . . you afraid that if we got to know each other you might like me, or something?'

'I don't dislike you now,' she protested. 'Only this damnable habit you have of asking irrelevant questions about equally irrelevant subjects.'

'Marriage is not an irrelevant subject,' he replied, for the first time actually raising his voice to meet hers.

'Well, it certainly is between you and me!' Justine yelled back. 'If you want to talk about marriage why don't you go and find somebody who's interested in marriage, like . . . oh . . . Possum!'

'Aha! Now the penny drops.' Wyatt's every word dripped insinuation. 'A little of the old green-eyed monster, eh? Turn around here and let's see the colour of your eyes, dear Justine.'

'I will not! And how dare you suggest that I'm . . . jealous? That's the most conceited thing I've ever heard!' Justine raged, and then shut up because she would have been incoherent with sheer frustration had she continued.

His reply came in a deliberately smarmy voice. 'Methinks the lady doth protest too much.'

Lips clamped shut, Justine turned away to stare out the side window. To hell with him, she thought. Let him talk to himself.

But Wyatt simply ignored her tantrum and continued talking as if he was sure she was listening. 'Actually, I'd have no objection to you working if we were married,' he told her. 'But only until the children started coming. Two of them, I think, provided we could manage one of each. Of course I know that aspect of things is purely up to me, and if I didn't get it right I suppose we could stretch it to four kiddies. Or is that too many, do you think?'

He didn't wait for an answer, obviously not expecting one. 'No, four wouldn't be too many. Especially if we could manage two sets of twins. Are there any twins in your family, Justine? Yes? No? Maybe? My, what delightful children they'd be if they inherited your quiet disposition. Not a word out of them during those long winter evenings . . . I can just see you, a little bundle of joy on each arm . . .'

'Damn you! Stop it! Just stop it!' she shouted, turning from the window to glare at him with eyes that definitely blazed green, although from anger, not jealousy.

'That's better,' he replied with infuriating calmness. 'I never could stand a complacent woman.'

'If you weren't driving this car I'd give you *complacent* where it would do you the most good,' Justine threatened, her voice a whisper of sneering rage.

'No sooner said than done,' Wyatt replied, abruptly wheeling the heavy automobile off into an all-too-convenient lay-by.

Justine shrank back against her side of the car, eyes

wary as she readied herself to repel his next move. But
Wyatt only leaned back against his own door, arms
folded arrogantly across his chest.

The two of them sat, unmoving but locked by their
eyes, for what seemed like hours to Justine but
was more realistically only a matter of minutes.
Characteristically, it was Wyatt who finally broke the
stalemate.

'Hummph!' he muttered half under his breath, and
without another word, reached forward to place the
heavy car into gear once more, steering carefully back
out on to the highway without so much as another
glance at his befuddled passenger.

Nor did he have much to say during the short remainder of the trip back to his restaurant. He enquired
once if Justine was getting cool, and once if she minded
him smoking as he drove. Nothing else.

It was, she decided, distinctly puzzling. What had
he expected from her—a screaming, hair-pulling
physical assault? Tears? A tantrum? She simply didn't
know.

Where she had been in quite an angry rage, her mood
now shifted entirely. She felt, somehow, that she had
failed him in some intangible way. And it worried her.
What worried her even more, however, was that she
should care one way or another *what* Wyatt thought
about her reaction to him. It was maddening that this
arrogant, sarcastic man should be so easily able to
manipulate her emotions within a single day of meeting
him.

A radio control mechanism opened the garage doors
at the restaurant when they arrived, so it was within
the moonlit shadows of the garage interior that Wyatt
strolled round the car to help Justine disembark.

His very touch, she found, was quite sufficient to
send her pulse racing, create an unexpected and heady
lightness of breath, an almost teenage clumsiness.
Silently he led the way to a narrow courtyard and a

rear door leading into the building, only freeing her arm
when he was required to use his key to admit them both.

Still in silence, he took her arm again, leading her
unerringly through darkened corridors and finally up
a set of stairs. At the top, he flipped on a light switch
and then carried on to the door of her apartment, where
he stood in haughty alertness until she had handed him
the door key and let him open the door for her. He
stepped in ahead of her, eyes scanning the mirrored
room, then as quickly retreated, offering only an abrupt
'Goodnight' as he turned away down the hallway.

Justine stood where he had left her, a living statue
whose trembling lower lip was mirrored a dozen times
from the walls around her. She was hurt, an obvious
enough reaction to the rudeness of his leavetaking. But
more, she was simply confused by it all.

It wasn't until anger began to override her tender-
ness of ego that she finally moved, flinging her handbag
down with a snarl and then flinging her evening cape
just as viciously after it.

'Damn! Damn . . . damn . . . damn . . . damn!' she
cried softly. 'What a dirty, stinking way to end a
beautiful evening. Oh, Wyatt Burns, I hate you!
Arrogant, self-centred, conceited, rotten *bastard*! If I
ever cook anything for you again it'll be laced with
arsenic. Pure, unadulterated rat poison—just exactly
what you deserve!'

Oblivious to the mirrors in her anger, Justine slung
off her clothing, flinging the dress to crumple over the
back of a chair, crumpling her hose into a formless
ball and carelessly tossing them into a corner. Then
she strode into the bathroom and diligently scrubbed
away her make-up, meeting her own angry eyes in the
mirror with a haughty disdain as her mind conjured
up revenges too radical for words.

Then, finally, she threw herself into the huge bed,
expecting to be kept awake all night by her anger, but
asleep too quickly to be surprised.

She was only marginally less angry when she came awake just after dawn with a sense of disorientation that lasted only a moment.

Showered and shampooed, her hair wrapped in a turban of towelling and her body crying out for nourishment, she was just belting on her robe when a soft knock at the door startled her.

'Who is it?' she called out suspiciously, fingers all a-fumble as she tried to remember the complicated operation of the spy-hole Wyatt had shown her.

'Possum,' came the reply, so quickly she no longer needed to see. Justine flung open the door to admit the slender singer-dancer-kitchen hand, dressed this morning in a pale ivory cat-suit and balancing a large tray in one small hand.

Possum stepped into the room, passing the surprised Justine with barely a glance as her eyes darted around the room. 'So this is the famous mirror room,' she said, eyes roving from image to image as she spun, complete with tray, through a full circle. 'God, you'd have to be brave to get your gear off in a place like this! It'd give me the creeps, no worries.'

Then her eyes took in the evidence of Justine's hasty disrobing of the night before, and widened just a bit as she turned to look at her.

'I *thought* you might be having a bit of a tiff with the lord of the manor,' she grinned. 'Hope it wasn't on account of me. Anyway, he's not too angry; he sent me up with your brekkie.'

'He what?' Justine couldn't quite take it in. After Wyatt's chilling departure, it was the last thing she might have expected.

'Brekkie—you know, toast, coffee, that sort of thing? Even tea, if you'd rather. He didn't seem to know what you'd want, exactly.'

Justine's mind whirled, but her stomach had no such confusion. It simply screamed for tea so loudly she had to obey.

'Lord, yes,' she sighed. 'Come and have some with me, unless he's got you doing something else.'

'Love to. I've only had coffee so far this morning,' Possum replied, gliding over to set down the tray on the small kitchenette table.

The two girls sat in silence long enough to get through that first cup—tea for Justine and coffee for Possum, then Justine flipped open the serving dish to find not only toast, but bacon, two eggs and some hash-browned potatoes.

'My goodness,' she protested, 'I can't possibly eat all this!' But she did, while Possum kept up a running commentary that began with a quite unexpected apology.

'And I'm apologising purely for me,' she said. 'We'll just ignore the fact that both Sebastian and his lordship threatened me with horrible punishments. But I just couldn't help myself yesterday. You were sitting there, and you looked so . . . so . . .'

'Gullible?' Justine prompted through a mouthful of egg.

'Yeah, that'll do. But it was really my fault. I've got an awful sense of humour—everybody says so. And then last night . . . well . . .' She giggled softly, almost spilling her second cup of coffee. 'If you could have seen your face when I walked out on that stage . . . it was priceless! I thought you were going to faint or something, for a minute. I just about broke up. And Wyatt . . . once he realised something was up. Oh, if looks could kill I wouldn't be here now!'

Wyatt? Justine had no memory of him being that way at all. If anything, she thought, the looks he'd been directing towards Possum were anything but killing.

'Too right,' Possum continued, correctly reading Justine's expression 'There are times I reckon he's got no sense of humour at all, although he has, of course. It's just not quite the same as most people's. After all, look at this place. To put you in here shows he's either got a sense of humour or he fancies you like anything. I mean, most of us have never even *seen* this suite.'

'That's strange,' Justine mused half to herself. 'I'm sure he told me the other head chefs had been quartered here.'

'And pigs do fly,' Possum laughed. 'This whole wing is Wyatt Burns' private domain . . . he'd no more have had any male chef, much less the last one we had, living here than fly to the moon.'

And with that pearl of wisdom she flung herself to her feet and headed for the door. 'I'm off now,' she said quite unnecessarily. 'See you in the kitchen when you're ready. Armand—he's your Number Two—is already there getting the provisioning under control.'

'Oh, great. Just what I need is to be thought late on my very first day,' Justine sighed. 'Take this tray with you, if you don't mind. I'll be there in . . . oh, twenty minutes maximum.'

'Don't hassle it,' Possum replied with a wry grin. 'The guy you're replacing never showed until ten o'clock at the absolute earliest, and nobody ever complained about it.'

'Perhaps not, but then he isn't here any more either,' Justine rejoined.

'Yes, but it had nothing to do with his starting times. Word is he got sacked because Wyatt thought he was paying too much attention to Gloria—that's Gloria Calder, the hostess here, if you want to be generous with your descriptions. Now if Wyatt had installed *her* in here,' and she waved expansively around the mirrored room, 'well, let's just say nobody'd have been too surprised. She's been trying hard enough and long enough to get herself installed next door, if you know what I mean. Anyway, she's been on holidays for a week, won't be back till next week, I think. And no sooner was she gone than Wyatt lowered the boom on the chef you're replacing.'

Turning towards the door again, she retreated long enough to grab up the breakfast tray, then swung round for one parting comment. 'I can't wait to see *her* face when she sees you!'

'It was a feeling Justine couldn't quite share, she thought as she rushed through her toilette and got into her working clothes to begin her day in the kitchen.

The rest of the morning sped past in a blur of introductions, unfamiliar faces and the sheer hard work of trying to fit herself into the established routine of the Wyatt's kitchen. Justine was wise enough to realise that in the beginning it would be she who would have to adapt; only a fool would try to walk into a successful operation waving a big stick and demanding all sorts of changes.

Her Number Two, a burly French-Canadian named Armand Duplessis, shaped up immediately as one of her major problems. His condescending attitude upon introduction had rapidly deteriorated into one of outright hostility, and made it abundantly obvious that he had expected to be awarded the job Justine had been given.

Not surprising. Indeed, Justine would have been more surprised if he hadn't been hostile, but she nonetheless considered it a major priority to try and win him round to her support.

Clearly she had no such worries with Possum, and the various kitchen hands and waitresses and waiters she met during the day seemed, if nothing else, neutral.

All but the head waiter, who was perhaps the biggest surprise of all, in his own unique way. Sebastian proved, to Justine's surprise, to be the classic, archetypal English butler, which should have accounted for Possum's cunning grin when she introduced him to Justine, but somehow didn't . . . quite.

He seemed . . . strangely familiar, but it wasn't until

he divested his plummy English accent and manners for just a moment, plummeting into a classic Greco-English patois to ask how she had enjoyed dinner the evening before, that it all fell into place.

'Zorba!' Justine cried in unfeigned delight. 'Oh, and you were, perfectly.' So this, she thought, explained Wyatt's comments about Possum's talents and his prediction: 'You haven't seen Sebastian at his best, either.'

'Yes, madam,' he replied, once again in the butler mould. 'And if I may be so bold, madam, may I enquire if my wife's apology this morning was satisfactory?'

Wife? Justine was absolutely floored. She stood there, mouth open but wordless, for so long that the incomparable actor before her got a very worried look in his eye.

Then, before she could speak, he turned and bellowed something in Greek, something long and ominous-sounding but in which the only word Justine could recognise was 'Parthenia!' What followed when Possum finally arrived would have qualified as classic Greek comedy if it hadn't been so obvious that Sebastian was serious. He waved his hands, shook his fists, cried oaths (or at least Justine presumed they were oaths) to the skies and stamped his feet.

But just as Justine, horrified by her own part in the assault, was about to speak out, Possum leaned over to kiss her husband softly on the mouth, stopping everything abruptly.

'Isn't he sweet?' she cooed to Justine as she tossed up her head and sauntered back to wherever she had come from.

Justine fully expected Sebastian-Zorba to explode with rage at that point, but he only shrugged, eyes alight with inner laughter.

'And I am, too,' he chuckled, holding out his hand to grasp Justine's and shake it heartily. 'Welcome to chaos, Justine.' Whereupon he kissed her heartily on both cheeks and whispered in her ear, 'I just hope you're not all uptight and disapproving like that French devil over there.'

A whisper, of course, that was just loud enough so that Armand couldn't help but hear it. The frustrated, angry glare he threw at Sebastian would have slain a lesser man, but Sebastian, as the butler, stalked haughtily back to his dining rooms without a backward glance.

'Animals!' Armand sneered. 'Nothing but frustrated, no-talent animals!'

He swung himself around and ploughed through the swinging doors, only to rebound from the arriving form of Wyatt himself, a Wyatt whose thunderous countenance as he watched the departing French-Canadian did nothing for Justine's already questionable serenity.

'You're off to a fine start, I see,' he glowered. 'What the hell's going on down here? I could hear the rumpus all the way up to my office!'

'Rumpus? There wasn't any rumpus,' she replied with faked calmness. 'Just . . . just a little staff discussion, that's all. I'm certainly sorry if it bothered you.'

'It didn't bother me, but it obviously bothered *him*,' Wyatt snapped, thumbing a gesture at the door which still swung from the second cook's exit. 'I suppose now I'll be advertising to replace him, tomorrow?'

'I most sincerely hope not,' Justine replied, biting at her lower lip to stop it trembling.

'And so you damn well should,'·he threatened, eyes like coals burning into her own. 'Because it'd be a toss-up which position I'd be advertising. Understood?'

'Perfectly! Now if you don't mind, our first lunch guests should be here any minute,' she replied waspishly, and was greatly surprised when he took her unsubtle hint and retreated from the kitchen without another word.

More important, to her great delight, he stayed out of her kitchen for the next three days, days which she found absolutely vital in her bid to establish an acceptable working relationship with all the other staff.

Armand, of course, was the only major problem. Justine quickly became tired of his arrogance and near-insolence, but short of throwing herself on his mercy?—and pleading, she just couldn't figure out how to swing him to her support without a major confrontation.

But with the arrival—and departure—of the butcher's van on the third day, matters foamed to a head with a speed that left her little choice of positive action.

It was just on three o'clock, and Justine was working in her little alcove office with one ear cocked for the distinctive sound of the butcher's van. She had asked Armand earlier to advise her on the man's arrival, because she had plans for a rather lengthy discussion with whoever was supplying them with fresh meat.

How she missed the van's arrival, she didn't know, but when she was startled by the van's horn screeching out its habitual farewell, she reared up from her chair in anger. Damn Armand! She knew full well he had deliberately ignored her instructions and was obviously spoiling for a direct confrontation, and now he'd get it.

She barely held herself in control as she strode into the main kitchen area to find the juniors all busy with their own work and Armand nowhere in sight. Then she followed one of the juniors' eyes to the rear door, and found her second in command bent over the box of freshly-delivered meat.

She sucked in a deep breath, only too conscious of the eyes following her as she walked quietly through the door and stood, silently, watching Armand sorting out the meat.

Her voice, when she finally spoke, was soft and quiet and very, very cold. 'I thought I asked you to advise me of the butcher's visit,' she demanded.

Armand, surprised by her presence, straightened abruptly. But his eyes were shuttered and watchful, hiding his habitual insolence for once.

'I thought it best not to disturb you, madam,' he said then, in a voice colourless but infuriating.

Justine fought back a biting reply, forcing her face to show none of the anger she felt. Instead, she looked him up and down, exactly, she thought, like a butcher inspecting a side of beef. A slightly raised eyebrow registered silent disapproval of the stain on his tunic front, and his vanity flared quickly.

He opened his mouth to say something, but Justine was too quick for him. In the same soft voice she asked politely, 'Don't you like working here, Armand?'

His mouth dropped open; for a second he was flummoxed, then recovered. 'Of course,' he replied. 'I enjoy very much working for Wyatt.' Not Wyatt's, nor even, Justine noticed, *Mr* Wyatt. She bit her tongue.

Looking around, eyes roving over the greenery of the surroundings, the soft lines of the outbuildings, she waited a moment, then spoke in a deliberately idle tone.

'I'm glad,' she said. 'Having people who enjoy their work is very important to a house like this, with such a high reputation to maintain . . . in all things.' And she stared again at the stain on his tunic, revelling in the flush which rose to his cheeks. 'I've been meaning to mention, by the way, how very pleased I've been with your sauces. A light, capable touch, like yours I haven't encountered since I left Paris.'

Again he flushed, but Justine wasn't sure if it was because of the compliment . . . or because he'd just realised she might actually understand some of the French—rude—things he'd muttered about her in her hearing.

But whatever else he had been expecting, she realised, it certainly wasn't a compliment. He was definitely confused now, and she leapt in while she still held the upper hand. 'I'm also very pleased at how thoroughly you've been instructing the juniors,' she continued. 'It isn't every chef who has the confidence to ensure that his underlings get the very best of instruction. Most are too afraid of being usurped. Why, one of the best that I ever knew in Paris was afraid to take a day off, for fear that one of the younger chefs would steal his position. And he certainly didn't have your flair for instruction, or at least not the nerve to risk imparting all his knowledge where it might be turned against him.'

Then she abruptly dropped the subject like a hot brick. Asking Armand to bring the meat cartons into the kitchen, she turned and preceded him without waiting to see his reaction. It wasn't until she'd opened the first carton and begun to inspect it that she spoke again.

'My God! Look at this . . . just look at it!' she stormed. 'If that's veal I'm a Jersey bull—in fact I wouldn't be surprised·if that's what *this* is.' She turned to the second chef with indignation written all over her face.

'Damn it, Armand, what does this fellow think he's dealing with—a couple of amateurs? I won't have my reputation, or yours, put on the line by serving this . . . this junk. Obviously my . . . predecessor must have picked out his own meat; I can't imagine you accepting stuff like this.'

Which was no lie. Whatever Armand's personal faults he was a perfectionist in his work, and Justine knew it.

She'd been less than impressed with the meat she'd been working with during that first few days, but had little choice but to use it. But this . . . this was of even poorer quality, she found after ripping open the rest of the cartons.

'I think,' she said, 'that it's high time this butcher was put in his place. It's an insult to this restaurant . . . and to *us* . . . and I don't intend to put up with it.'

'I am with you, madame,' agreed Armand, and the sincerity in his voice so elated Justine that she turned away on the pretext·of further examination to hide that elation from her new-won supporter.

'There isn't even an invoice with this,' she snapped. 'Now I don't like that . . . not one bit.'

'There would not be,' Armand replied. 'All the invoices in the past have gone directly to Miss Calder, I believe.'

'Right! Well, that's another thing that'll be changed,' Justine said angrily. 'There's just no way I'm going to have *us* responsible for anything we can't control. Would you please pack this stuff back up; I've got a phone call or two to make.'

It took her ten minutes on the telephone to line up a new meat supplier, one she knew to be reliable and probably even cheaper than the one she was about to dismiss. And another five minutes had the former butcher's bewildered assistant assuring her that yes, he would inform the boss that this order was unacceptable and was to be retrieved by the butcher that very day.

An hour later her new supplies arrived, but it was nearly five before the old butcher arrived in his noisy van.

Justine thrust back her shoulders and drew several deep breaths before calmly asking Armand to bring out the unaccepted meat, then going out herself to meet the butcher at his van.

The man was leaning negligently against one mudguard, his white dustcoat soiled and his unkempt appearance quite enough to make Justine shudder inside. They had been buying meat from this?

'Understand you got a complaint, missy,' the man sneered in a whiny, abrasive voice.

'I have,' she nodded, then gestured for Armand to place the cartons in the back of the van for inspection.

As he did so, the butcher ignored him entirely, focusing his piggy little eyes instead on Justine. She felt as though a thousand insects were walking on her skin as the man not only mentally undressed her, but committed unspeakable indignities on her as well.

His attitude changed immediately, however, once she had staved off his leer sufficiently to begin her lengthy dissertation on the lack of quality in his products. His eyes grew hard and angry, his cheeks flushed defensively.

'. . . and therefore I've changed butchers,' she concluded, meeting his eyes with her own filled with anger and contempt.

'You just hold on there, missy,' he raged in an ugly tone. 'We got a contract and I'm going to hold you to it. You take my meat or I'll be seeing you in court! Is that clear?'

Justine glared back at him, repulsed both by his manner and his slovenly appearance.

'I doubt very much if your shop could stand a health department examination,' she said calmly, 'and certainly this van could not. I have a friend there whose advice I'll be seeing·on that subject first thing in the morning. But it really isn't important anyway, from the point of view of any legalities between us, since I'm assured that your . . . contract . . . was on a week-to-week basis in any event.'

'The hell it was . . .' he began, but she cut him off.

'And since I have no intention of ordering another thing from you, I think that about sums it up,' she said haughtily. 'If you wish to sue, of course, that's your privilege.'

The butcher's face was livid, heavy drinker's veins flushed with anger and the whisky she could smell on him under the sour odour of his clothing.

'Listen, you great cow . . .' he began, only to cut off the insult abruptly as Armand stepped suggestively closer, his stocky frame alert and his eyes wary.

'Don't . . . Armand; you'd only get your uniform dirty,' Justine snorted, noticing the immediate retreat in the butcher's tiny eyes. 'We wouldn't want to have to decontaminate you.'

The butcher took the hint; he abandoned the affair and sauntered insolently back to the driver's seat of his van after slamming the rear doors.

'I'll be having words with Miss Calder about this,' he jeered. 'And then you'll see what's what!'

CHAPTER FOUR

SCALDING tears of pure nervousness flooded Justine's eyes as the butcher's van squealed out of the driveway. She turned, stumbled, and would have fallen but for Armand catching her in his arms.

There were no sexual overtones to his support as he helped her over the threshold and back into the kitchen area, and she strove to thank him warmly, shaking away the tears as best she could.

Her eyes cleared, he released her immediately, but as Justine looked up, she realised only too quickly just why.

'Interesting,' drawled Wyatt Burns in a voice so chilling, so alive with bitter sarcasm that Justine winced at the force of it. 'I suppose this is some new kind of French provincial cooking,' he continued, his eyes thrusting Armand away and back to his duties, 'but let me remind you that this restaurant specialises in English delicacies. And that there are customers waiting.'

'I . . . but . . . I . . . oh, you don't understand,' Justine fumbled clumsily. Armand had prudently followed the orders in Wyatt's look, but she couldn't avoid the anger and the bitter accusation he was insinuating.

'Obviously,' he sneered. 'It's because I'm old, you see, and my eyes play tricks on me.'

'Well, they obviously do,' she snapped. 'If you'd just give me a chance, I could explain.'

'I shall. And you'd damned well better,' he snarled. 'But first, I suggest you attend to your work, which involves ensuring that the customers have the food they've ordered in a reasonable time. Or is that too much to ask, Miss Ryan?'

'No, it is not.'

'Fine. Then I suggest you get to it,' he snapped, and turned on his heel to storm away, the swinging door to the restaurant almost smashed from its hinges at his passing.

Justine got through the remainder of the evening somehow, but it was on pure reflex, intuitive knowledge. She didn't understand Wyatt's attack, felt sure she could straighten it out quickly and easily, but felt much less confident about having to explain the situation about the butcher.

Also, she had a scheme involving her junior chefs that she wanted desperately to initiate, having promised to do so provided he would approve, and tonight would be her best opportunity before the two-day closing to broach the subject. Hardly an auspicious moment for it, she thought.

Once the last of her own work was done in the kitchen, she left Armand to supervise the final desserts and cleaning up, slipped out of the smock she had taken to wearing instead of the more customary white trousers and blouse, and slipped up the back staircase to her room.

She felt grubby, smelly and genuinely fagged out, and determined that she would take time for a quick shower and change of clothes before obeying Wyatt's summons to his illustrious presence.

Refreshed, and comfortable but casual in tight-fitting jeans and a T-shirt, she was nonetheless trembling with nervousness when she knocked on his office door and opened it to his gruff command.

She stepped through, then stopped abruptly at finding herself face to face with a slim, elegantly-dressed brunette whose snapping dark eyes scoured over Justine and her casual clothing like an abrasive scrub-brush.

Justine nodded a welcome without waiting for an

introduction, but found her nod unreturned as the brunette stared right through her before turning back towards where Wyatt lounged on the window seat.

'I'll see you . . . later, then, darling,' the woman drawled, every word a sensual, sexual display that matched the body language she was telegraphing at the same time.

Wyatt didn't reply, didn't have to. The look in his eye, Justine thought, would have been quite sufficient. The brunette smiled, first at him and then, scornfully at Justine as she turned and shouldered her way past her.

'Sit down.' Wyatt's voice held no welcome for Justine. 'Do you want a drink?'

'I'll . . . get it,' she replied, stepping towards the drink cabinet without waiting for his approval. Before she realised he had moved, strong fingers clamped above her elbow and she was steered across to where he had been sitting.

'Brandy and lemonade, I presume?' he said with a raised eyebrow. 'Or would you prefer something . . . French, perhaps?'

'Actually, I'd prefer something with a little less sarcasm in it,' she retorted, eyes blazing with sudden anger. Who the hell did he think he was . . . God? The nerve of the man! He was deliberately setting out to get her goat, and, she realised as she met his eyes defiantly, he'd succeeded and knew it only too well.

'Well, it's French brandy, anyway,' he mused almost to himself, quite ignoring her remark.

His back was turned as he poured out the drink, but to Justine's eyes he was fairly shaking with laughter. She wished she had something to throw at him, and for an instant actually considered flinging the cushion beside her.

When he finally placed the drink in her fingers, she almost threw *that* back in his face, but thought better

of it immediately. A waste of good drink, she thought,
but oh, it would have been satisfying.

Wyatt picked up his own drink and settled com-
fortably on the other end of the settee, leaning back
into the corner of the structure in the casual attitude of
a man who knows he is totally in control of the situation.

'Cheers!' he said, lifting his glass in salute but showing no facial expression to match.

Justine lifted her own glass in silence. She was too
busy sifting through what she intended to say to this
arrogant, haughty figure. She took one sip of the drink,
then another, but Wyatt made no move to start the
conversation. He was, she decided, waiting for her.
And it'll be a long wait, she vowed silently.

She had almost finished her glass, sipping slowly
under his hooded, watchful gaze and desperately wishing herself somewhere, anywhere else, before he finally
broke the silence with a question that exploded out of
nowhere.

'Where the hell do you get off firing the butcher? On
whose authority?'

'On yours,' she replied simply after taking a moment
to rearrange her thoughts.

'Oh?' It was question and disagreement in a single
word.

'Yes . . . oh,' she retorted. 'Or did I misunderstand
when you told me to run my kitchen with full
authority—and responsibility—for the results?'

'I said that.' Not an argument, but not quite the
admission she would have liked. Damn the man for his
bland, unreadable voice.

'His meat was unacceptable. I found a better supplier and I fired him. End of story.' And make what
you want of that! she thought.

'You didn't think it might be advisable to consult
me first?'

'I didn't think it was necessary. It might very well

have been advisable, but there wasn't really time,' she replied.

'You seemed to have plenty of time for other things.' The sarcasm was a steady, venomous shroud around those words.

Justine took several slow, deep breaths. When she finally spoke, her voice—she hoped—was as impassive as his own.

'The man was nasty. I was upset, I stumbled, Armand kept me from falling and helped me inside. That's what you saw. Whatever you *thought* you saw, I have no control over,' she replied slowly.

'Maybe the man had a right to be nasty.'

'That man was born nasty! He's a foul, rancid little man, and what's more, he was cheating you. I'd stake my reputation on it,' Justine replied hotly.

'He was.' And what the hell is that, she wondered, an agreement, or what?

'He . . . was?' she finally queried, head cocked suspiciously to one side.

'He was . . . with a lot of help from my chef—make that former chef,' Wyatt replied grimly. 'But I'm sorry you fired him.'

'I don't understand.' And that, she mused, was the understatement of the week.

'Let's just say I'm pretty sure he had help.'

Armand! That was her first thought, but she rejected it immediately as unfair, and very likely unjust as well. Or was it? Could her second-in-command's quick about-face have been aimed more at saving his own skin than anything else?

'And I've queered your pitch,' she replied finally. 'I'm sorry, but I didn't know. And it was my responsibility to ensure that the quality of meat is . . .'

'Nobody's arguing about that.' Brutal, his voice. Cutting and abrupt. But why?

'Have you got anything else you plan on changing

around here?' he asked abruptly. And the tone said
very clearly, 'You'd better not.'

'Actually . . . yes,' Justine said cautiously. 'There's
one thing I'd quite like to try, provided of course you
agree. It's about Monday nights.'

'We're closed on Monday nights.'

'Well, I *know* that,' she retorted. Damn the
man . . . did he think her entirely stupid? Gamely, she
resolved to continue. 'We're closed, which means the
staff must either cook their own meals in their . . .
flats, or else go out to dinner. What I have in mind is
to make Monday nights the sole province of the junior
chefs—they have to be back anyway from their days
off—and let them cook for the rest of us as a sort of
training programme. We would all throw in to cover
the costs, except for the one chosen to cook, of course,
and it would give each of them an opportunity to really
show what they've learned.'

'Which means, I presume, that I also would be
expected to partake. What have you been doing, teach-
ing them every mushroom dish you know?'

Justine looked up in frank amazement. Was he trying
to be funny? Nothing in his facial expression said so.
Nor in his eyes, those fathomless, brooding black eyes
that seemed to consume her every time he focused
her with his haughty stare.

'I . . . had thought to let each of them choose
for themselves what they'd like to exhibit,' she
said.

'Hmm,' he muttered. 'We've got four in various
stages of apprenticeship, which means nobody should
get hit with the job too often. Are they all willing?'

'Yes. And there would actually be five, because
Possum's expressed an interest as well,' said Justine,
bracing herself for the explosion.

'Possum?' And for the first time, his face cracked
from its stolid expression; he fairly dissolved in a burst
of laughter. 'My God!' he said finally. 'You expect to

feed the entire staff on boiled water . . . and probably undercooked at that?'

'That's horrid,' Justine accused, eyes flashing as she leapt to her friend's defence. During the past week she'd finally—she hoped—got Possum and her tall tales in some kind of perspective, and she liked her more each day.

'But true!'

'It is *not* true, and I don't know how you can justify saying such a thing,' Justine snapped in reply. 'Or do you presume, perhaps, to know my staff's capabilities better than I do?'

'*My* staff, I might point out,' he said unequivocally. 'And certainly, my dear Justine, I can presume to know my own sister better than you ever will—I've been saddled with her long enough.'

'Your . . . sister!' Justine was dumbfounded. It sounded all too much like one of Possum's elaborate little tales, although even more ridiculous than when Possum had claimed her husband to actually be her father.

Wyatt grinned, a wicked, wolfish, the-better-to-eat-you-with grin that was so close to being a smirk it might well have been. 'You don't believe me, do you?'

'With . . . Possum, I'm never sure what to believe,' Justine admitted. 'And with a real name like Parthen . . .' Her voice droned off when she saw the look in his eyes, definitely humorous this time.

'That,' he said quite seriously, 'is what Sebastian calls her. His *sweet virgin*. Very likely because her real name is Pomona, which is Latin for *fertile*, which is about the only damned thing dear Possum hasn't yet managed. When she does, I'd be amazed at anything less than triplets, and I can only hope and pray that Sebastian's got his Greek *taverna* totally under control by then so I don't have to put up with being uncle-cum-babysitter for them all.'

Justine was honestly astounded. It simply didn't make any sense, and therefore was undoubtedly true.

That, she'd discovered, was the way with Possum. She had already found out that the girl was actually three years older than herself, and that she had been married to Sebastian for the last seven years, almost since he'd first come to Wyatt's as a head waiter. There had also been a number of other confidences . . . but *this*!

Wyatt seemed to be reading her mind. Abruptly, he rose and strode to his desk, stabbing at the intercom. 'Send Possum up here, please,' he directed whoever was at the other end.

'Oh, but . . .' Justine's objections were overridden.

Wyatt merely pointed his finger at her in a distinct order for silence, then strolled over to refill their glasses. He was sitting across from Justine when a light knock sounded at the door and Possum sauntered in without waiting for his call.

'You rang, master?' she queried, dipping in a flourish of curtsey.

'Why haven't you told Justine you're my sister?' he demanded without preamble.

'Humph! You surely wouldn't expect me to admit it?' she countered haughtily, swinging easily into the role of astonished innocent.

'And why not? Ignoring, of course, that I keep you and your asinine husband in jobs, give you a place to live, and have probably paid for most of that Greek chophouse with what you steal from my kitchen.'

Possum blithely ignored both the accusation and the tone, which to Justine's ears sounded menacing in the extreme.

'You have no sense of humour,' she retorted, flinging back her shoulders and tossing her head to one side in a gesture that should have reminded Justine of some movie star or another, but didn't.

'Ohh! Why do I bother?' Wyatt asked in apparent disgust. 'Take yourself back to your scullery, wench, before I lose my temper.'

'Certainly, master.' Possum repeated her curtsey,

this time to Justine as well, and withdrew.

Wyatt shook his head. 'Sense of humour? How the hell could anybody have a sense of humour with that for a sister? And Sebastian's at least as bad. I'd run them both off in a minute if he wasn't so damned talented and she wasn't my only sister,' he raged.

Justine said nothing. She didn't, in fact, dare to open her mouth lest the laughter she was so desperately trying to throttle break free and fan Wyatt's anger to even greater fury.

She tried to take a sip of her drink, and almost choked as it met the laughter and tried to change direction in mid-throat. Wyatt's scowl did nothing to make it easier. Justine wanted desperately to escape before she broke up entirely, but she couldn't flee without a word, and to speak would be to laugh.

'It's allowed, you know.' Wyatt's voice now was strangely soft, almost caressing. Then his lip curled into something approaching a grin before he literally shouted at her: 'Go ahead and laugh, damn it! I would, if I were you.'

Justine barely managed to set down her nearly empty glass before she exploded, her eyes filling with tears as the laughter welled up in her throat, choking off any possibility of a quick return to sanity. She laughed so hard she almost fell off the settee, and through the tears she could see Wyatt striding over to refill their glasses yet again. *He* wasn't laughing, she noticed, which somehow made it all seem even more hilarious, but eventually she got things vaguely under control and sat apprehensively facing him as she choked down her final chuckles.

'I much prefer you laughing to when you're angry,' he said then. 'You have a very open, honest laugh, without vindictiveness.'

'I'm . . . not a very vindictive person, I don't think,' she replied. What was he getting at now?

He sipped slowly at his drink, only his eyes in direct

communication as they roved caressingly over her face.
'Have you come to terms with all the mirrors yet?' he
asked without any warning.

'I . . . er . . . yes. Sort of,' she said. It was true, in a
way. She'd simply draped spare towels, clothing,
whatever was handiest, over the most offensive of
them. Only the huge one over the bed, impossible to
disguise or cover up without a major effort, caused her
any serious trauma.

'I'll bet you've covered most of them up,' he said,
and Justine fancied that one corner of his mouth had
quirked, ever so slightly, into a tiny grin.

'Either you're a very good guesser or you've been
spying,' she replied. 'Everything I've done is purely
makeshift, though. I've done nothing permanent or
damaging.'

'I should certainly hope not,' he replied. But she
couldn't tell if it was a compliment or a simple statement of fact. 'And how about the menu?' he asked in a
total switch of subject. 'Are you happy with it, or do
you have big changes planned there as well?'

The radical shifting from subject to subject made
Justine feel quite ill at ease, and she hesitated before
answering that.

'I . . . have a few ideas, yes,' she finally admitted.
'But not right now. I'd like quite a bit more time to
become quite thoroughly familiar with the present
menu before suggesting any changes or additions.'

'Ah.' He looked down into his glass. 'From that, I
presume that I might be consulted on such matters?'

'Well, of course! You hired me to cook, not to go
about reorganising your entire operation.' Justine
wasn't as indignant as she appeared, but his innuendo
was distasteful.

'Oh, I know that,' he replied. 'I just wanted to see if
you still knew it. In addition to having . . . no sense of
humour, I don't much like surprises. Not that kind, at
any rate.'

And what did he expect her to say to that? Justine simply couldn't think of an appropriate reply from her own viewpoint, so instead of bothering, she gulped down the remainder of her drink and rose to her feet.

'It's late,' she said. 'I've had a hard day and tomorrow will be just a repeat of it, so if you don't mind I think I'll say goodnight.' And then some malicious inner devil took hold of her tongue, and she added, 'Besides, I seem to remember you have another appointment yet this evening.'

Wyatt's eyes flashed momentarily, then a curtain dropped over them, hiding all expression. 'Yes,' he said quite slowly, speculatively. 'Yes, I have, haven't I? Goodnight, Justine. Sleep well.'

It was total dismissal, but as she strolled back up to her reflective suite, Justine couldn't be totally sure about her own feelings in the matter. She was tired, or at least she had been until he had so abruptly turned off, leaving her to depart a room that seemed already empty of him despite his quite obvious physical presence.

'What did you expect, for goodness' sake, a goodnight kiss?' she muttered angrily to herself as she fitted the elaborate key into her door. 'You're letting him get to you, my girl, and you're forgetting that Wyatt Burns is a man to take full advantage of such a thing. He does it deliberately.'

Justine undressed and flung herself face down in the huge, canopied bed, unwilling to face the reflection in the big mirror overhead. The night before, she had lain there making faces at herself until sleep took her; tonight such an exercise was ludicrous in the extreme.

And even face down in her pillows she kept seeing images, most of them tall and lean, with sooty, hooded dark eyes that could reveal everything . . . or nothing. She needed no photograph to hold Wyatt's image; it was burned into her memory by forces she couldn't control, and the realisation was sobering.

Tonight there was another image as well, one that sprang to virulent life when Justine heard the door close loudly in the suite next to her own. Wyatt's suite, the inside of which she had never seen, but in which she was sure the hard-eyed brunette was a welcome visitor. Gloria Calder had revealed a most self-assured familiarity with Wyatt.

She recalled the way Gloria had been able to look straight through her, as if Justine simply didn't exist in the slender woman's world at all. 'Which probably I don't,' she mused half aloud. Certainly Gloria had a suave elegance that Justine never hoped to achieve, almost an artificial brilliance, but one she couldn't hope to outshine. She brought to mind the women of Paris, to whom style was an end in itself.

She realised, suddenly, that she was once again guilty of making quite bold assumptions. Who said the slender brunette was Gloria Calder? They hadn't been introduced. Justine reached back through her memory; had Wyatt given any indication of his lovely visitor's identity? He had not.

'But it was Gloria Calder, I'd stake my job on it,' she muttered to herself only moments before sleep came.

She was less certain by morning, especially since the lady in question never put in any sort of appearance throughout that frantic Friday or on the hectic Saturday that followed it. The kitchen crew worked flat out during those two days, with full-house bookings and several obviously important diners who hadn't booked, but were fitted in as early departures allowed space.

The only consolation, Justine thought, was her own growing satisfaction with the job and Armand's continued evidence of his new allegiance to her. No longer sulky, no longer insolent in any way, he was instead the perfect second-in-command, taking and delegating authority as required and working fully as hard as she.

On Sunday—beautiful, peaceful, non-working Sunday—Justine spent most of the day doing absolutely nothing but laze beside the swimming pool, soaking up the sun and forcing herself to relax. Monday was even better; she didn't have to force herself, but joined happily in the pool games with the various staff members who also used the pool extensively on those days the restaurant was closed.

It was heavenly, and she determined to take advantage of Wyatt's offer and get in a quick swim each morning. It was, she thought, exactly what she needed to get a good start on her working days.

Tuesday it was back to work as normal, and on that day and throughout the next few weeks—except for one single incident—Justine threw herself pleasurably into a routine that worked like a dream. Even that one incident, she decided almost as soon as it was over, was hardly anything that could take the shine off a truly splendid job.

It had occurred on Tuesday morning, when Justine was busily planning the coming week's menu changes. She had been sitting at her desk in the alcove, struggling with the various possibilities from the list of things Wyatt had decreed as suitable alternatives, when a slight sound behind her made her turn in surprise.

Gloria Calder! By this time Justine knew that it was indeed she who had been in Wyatt's office that evening, but she had hardly set eyes on the woman since, and presumed she was still on holiday.

Justine rose, a friendly smile on her face as she made to introduce herself, but a second look at the slender, dark-haired woman's eyes made her less enthusiastic than she might have been.

'You'll be Gloria Calder, of course,' she began. 'I'm . . .'

'I know who you are,' was the rude interjection. 'I'd like the kitchen accounts, if you don't mind.'

Charming! I'm so glad you're going to be friendly,

Justine thought. Get out of the wrong side of the bed this morning? And whose bed, I wonder? Aloud, she said nothing, but knitted her eyebrows together as she began to try and figure out Gloria's demand.

'Are you deaf or something?' The voice was viperish, a sibilant, hissing, haughty voice that immediately put Justine on edge.

'Not that I'm aware of,' she replied calmly. 'May I enquire just *why* you want my accounts?'

'I do all the accounts for this house, that's why,' was the surly reply. 'And I'm very busy, so would you just get me what I've asked for, without a whole lot of backchat.'

Justine choked down the red fury that threatened to make her slash out at this hostile, disdainful and rude woman. 'No,' she said very softly, 'I don't think so. I don't know how it's worked in the past, Miss Calder, but my understanding is that the kitchens are my responsibility, and of course that covers the accounting as well.'

'May I point out, *Miss* Ryan, that keeping the accounts is my job, and that I certainly don't need any assistance from a . . . a cook!' Gloria spat out the final word as if it tasted bad. 'The system as it is has worked admirably with every cook here before you, and it will still function when you're gone, which I understand will be in three weeks anyway. Surely you don't expect me to initiate a whole new system just for your *temporary* stay here?'

Justine felt her stomach heave. In the pleasantness of her first week, things had gone so well that she had quite forgotten that she was still on trial. Then anger took charge, and she answered coldly but firmly. 'I am not in the least concerned what systems you initiate. Part of my job is inventory control and I intend to do it. Unless, of course, you'd like to call Mr Burns down and we'll get his decision here and now.'

'That will hardly be necessary,' was the terse reply.

'I shall speak to Wyatt myself. And while I'm at it, I'll speak to him about your attitude as well!'

Justine smiled, then widened the smile as she saw the look of apprehension on the other moman's face. Gloria couldn't see, as Justine could, Wyatt Burns stepping through the swinging doors to the kitchen.

'Oh, I think now is as good a time as any,' she said quietly, then waved. 'Excuse me! Could we have a moment of your time?'

'Any time,' he drawled. 'Morning, ladies. What's the problem?'

'Oh, it's no problem, Wyatt,' Gloria cooed. 'I was just explaining to Miss Ryan that she needn't bother with the kitchen accounts, as I do them with the others for the house.' Her voice was silky smooth and her eyes drank in every aspect of Wyatt's tall, lean figure as she visibly preened before him. Justine couldn't help but feel overshadowed in her jeans and T-shirt, comparing that outfit to Gloria's expensive and well-tailored pants-suit.

'And I suppose you'd prefer to do them yourself, Justine?' he asked in a voice that told her nothing at all.

'Yes, I would,' she replied. 'It's the best way to keep a running check on quality and ensure minimum wastage, and it helps me to ensure that our prices aren't shifted out of line by seasonal demands.'

'Considering the affair with that butcher, I think you're right,' he agreed, and Justine almost fainted at the lack of argument.

Gloria had no such problem. 'I've been meaning to mention that to you,' she said, speaking directly to Wyatt as if Justine wasn't even there. 'I had a quite distressing call this morning from our butcher, and I really don't know how such a misunderstanding could have occurred. He was most upset at the things Miss Ryan said to him, but I think I've managed to convince him to give us another chance. I mean, really, he's been serving us for years and years.'

'You may be right,' said Wyatt. 'But this isn't the place to discuss it. Come up to the office and we'll thrash it out there.'

Justine could only stand there with her mouth open. How could he? All the pleasure of her earlier victory spilled away, leaving her with only a bad taste in her mouth as Wyatt left the kitchen with Gloria hanging like a doll on his arm.

All that morning she waited for a summons that would let her know what decision had been made, but it wasn't until after the noon rush, and the regular Tuesday visit by the butcher she herself had chosen, that the summons finally came.

It was almost three o'clock when she knocked on the door of Wyatt's office and was admitted by his usual gruff summons. 'Come and sit down,' he growled. 'I'll be with you in a minute.'

Justine sat and watched as he quickly scratched his signature on some letters, his long, slender fingers slashing across the pages with a careless flourish.

'Right,' he said finally. 'The butcher . . .'

'I . . . I really thought that was settled,' she began. 'I've . . . well, the butcher I've engaged now really is much better. And cheaper.'

'And more reliable, as well, I suspect,' he said with a stern glance that shut her mouth. 'But that's not the point.'

'It isn't?'

'No.' His stern attitude was unreadable. 'The other fellow has been involved with us for a long time, as Gloria said. I want you to throw some of our business his way.'

'I see,' Justine replied. But she didn't see, not really. Was he going to totally ignore her recommendations . . . decisions?

'No, you don't,' he said then. 'And I'm not shrugging off your personal attitude on this, either.' Then, abruptly and quite surprisingly, he smiled at her, and Justine's heart leaped in her breast. 'Give him just enough to make it worth his time, but not so much that it isn't worth the time of your new chap. Understood?'

Justine shook her head. 'Not really,' she admitted. 'But of course I'll do exactly as you say.'

'Good girl,' he said, and she felt like a dog that had just done its party trick correctly. And it hurt, somehow. She lowered her eyes, then rose quickly and headed for the door without another word, only to be halted with her fingers reaching for the doorknob.

'Justine!' The command defied ignoring. She turned and looked back at him, head raised and hoping he wouldn't be able to see the tears forming. Wyatt's eyes were hard and penetrating when he spoke.

'Stop acting as if I've gone against you, because I haven't, not at all,' he told her. 'Just trust me; try and have a little faith.'

'If you say so.' She couldn't say more.

'And try not to bite the bastard when he comes,' Wyatt said with an unexpected grin. 'You won't have to put up with him long, only two or three weeks at best. Okay?'

She couldn't answer that. On the heels of Gloria's comment it was a confirmation of a death sentence. Two or three weeks! Just long enough to serve out her trial period.

The hurt and apprehension stayed with her throughout most of that day, but during those that followed Wyatt so often complimented her on her work, so often stepped into the kitchens only long enough for a smile, a quick word of encouragement to her or one of the apprentices, that she lost her apprehension quite quickly.

And now there was only a single week to go. The thought struck her as she lounged beside the pool, for once alone on a sunny Monday morning. One more week and then what? Would she be staying on? she wondered. Or going off to seek a new job, one without the challenge and satisfaction of Wyatt's . . . one without Wyatt himself?

That, Justine realised, was her real dilemma. It was no longer possible for her to deny that the prime attraction of her job was Wyatt Burns himself, not that the admission did her much good. Ever since that explosive kiss on her first meeting with him, he had been, if not a model of decorum, at least a respectable employer who kept his hands to himself. There had been no need for Justine to keep fending him off, an unpleasant aspect of some previous jobs she had held.

If anything, his interest in her seemed too purely one of business for her taste. Of course he had Gloria Calder to cater to his romantic needs, Justine thought. The slender brunette had made her claim abundantly clear on the few occasions they had spoken since the single dispute over the accounts.

Gloria's all-too-obvious dislike of Justine herself wasn't terribly upsetting. A bit puzzling, considering the fact that Wyatt had shown absolutely no sign of anything but a professional interest, but not really upsetting, Justine thought.

She still didn't understand his unexplained delegation of the mirrored suite to her personal use. It seemed much more logical to have installed Gloria there, instead of in her cottage unit with the other staff.

'Maybe she's already told him she can't stand the sight of herself,' Justine chuckled half aloud. 'Now *that* I could understand; maybe even sympathise with.'

'Do you always talk to yourself?' The unexpected voice—*his* voice, unmistakably—made Justine shiver, first with alarm, but then . . .

'Only when I want to be sure I'll like the answers,' she retorted, half turning and squinting into the sun as she looked up towards him.

Wyatt, like herself, wore only a swimsuit, and she

was immediately conscious of the powerful muscles on his lean but well-built figure.

'That makes sense, I suppose,' he grunted, dropping to sprawl uninvited at her side. 'And who are you sympathising with?'

Justine could hardly answer that one honestly, and was forced to remain silent while she tried to think up a suitable if untrue reply. Wyatt, however, gave her no real chance.

'Like that, is it?' he asked. 'What is it this time—something Possum's done, or your pseudo-French admirer?'

'He's not pseudo-French; he's French-Canadian as you very well know,' Justine replied without thinking. 'In any event, neither supposition is correct.'

'Well, at least you're not denying he's your admirer, not that you could, considering the way he follows you around like a puppy dog. Have you invited him up to inspect your mirrors yet?'

Justine gasped at the sneering tone of the question, as much as at the impertinence of it. She very nearly demanded to know just who the hell Wyatt Burns thought he was, asking such personal questions, then decided against it. An outright argument would serve no useful purpose.

'Well?' he demanded through her silence.

'It's certainly a lovely day, isn't it?' she responded brightly. 'But I think I'm getting too much sun; perhaps I'd best get indoors.'

'Easier to put on some sunscreen cream,' Wyatt countered. 'Lay down and I'll put it on for you.'

'I think not,' she hedged, only to find his hand forcing her down on to her towel.

'Do as you're told. I have things to say to you and I don't fancy missing *my* sunshine in the process,' he declared.

And before Justine could further object, she felt the chill as a pool of sunscreen cream was dribbled haphazardly down her back. Then strong yet somehow delicate fingers were at work spreading the cream across her shoulder blades, into the knobbly hollow beside her spine.

Wyatt's fingers had a tantalising eroticism to them as they alternately caressed and massaged her. It was as if he were blind, using his fingers as eyes to reveal to him all the external secrets of her.

She half reared up with a start when an unexpected tug released the string of her bikini, but as quickly realised she just couldn't get up, not now. Wyatt chuckled at her discomfiture.

When she tried to reach back and retie the strap, he casually flicked away her fingers. 'Just lie back and enjoy it, as the old saw goes,' he growled. 'Nobody's going to hurt you.'

'Easy for you to say,' she retorted. 'I do wish you'd stop this.'

'Stop what? This?' And his fingers traced a tingling line down her spine. 'Or this?' And they circled in a monotonous spiral in the soft hollow at the base of her spine, just above the edge of her bikini briefs. 'Or maybe this?' And they stroked in concentric movements that followed the thin white line of the bikini top, now so useless as the strings lay on the towel beside her. It was impossible to move as his light tracery slipped farther and farther down towards the swelling of her breasts.

Then, miraculously, thankfully, horribly, he stopped! The fingers moved, fresh cream dribbled lower down her back, and the sexuality gave way to a skilful manipulation as he wordlessly continued spreading the cream.

Justine's mind sighed with relief; her body screamed in anguish at the cessation of that tantalising torment. She wanted to speak, but dared not, lest her inner voice take control and reveal her true desires.

She shivered uncontrollably as his fingers moved

lower, caressing the soft swell of her hips and then
bypassing the edges of her bikini briefs to touch lightly
on the backs of her thighs, the tender skin behind her
knees, the narrowing at her ankles.

This time there was no attempt to disguise his ex-
ploration; every touch was a deliberate caress and each
touch produced in her a desire for more. As the cream
spread, softly fanning the flame of need in her, she
again had that sensation that Wyatt had closed his
eyes and was using only his fingers in a tactile ex-
ploration.

Along the inside of her leg those incredible fingers
moved, leaving a trail of desire along the swelling of
her calf, the curve of her knee, then upwards along the
softness of her inner thigh, moving inexorably towards
the very heart of her womanhood. Justine's mind,
almost a totally separate entity, could almost *see* the
progress of his fingers, bringing her entire body alive
with response.

If he touched her . . . there . . . she would be lost.
Already some inner demon was prodding at her
muscles, urging her body to turn over, to expedite his
caress, to open herself to him like a flower to the sun.
She trembled, not in fear but in a mute expectancy.

The muscles of her legs had disappeared; she was
like a rag doll, totally vulnerable to his touch, to his
every whim. The slightest pressure of those heavenly
fingers and her legs seemed to flow farther apart, easing
his access.

He could have her now, Justine knew. Even here in
the questionable seclusion of the pool surrounds, where
they could be interrupted at any moment. And she
wouldn't resist him; indeed she would help, would
come to him willingly, join her body to his with an
eagerness that was building in her like an infant tornado.

She felt, as if from a distance, the touch of his lips
near her ear, fancied she heard him whisper her name,

drawing it out in the continental fashion, softly, tenderly.

His lips touched her again, their warmth like a hot wind stirring the fires of her own desire as they traced a line across her cheek, and she twisted her head to meet them with her own lips.

Inside her, a tiny, isolated voice cried 'Madness!' against the tornado that reached out to enfold them both. Then another voice, far in the distance, intruded, and Wyatt's lips hissed a chilling, fearful reply.

CHAPTER FIVE

'Damn! Don't *move*, Justine.' And his fingers, now swift and sure in their movements, flew to re-tie the strings of her bikini top even as she returned to a semblance of normality and her ears recognised the sound of approaching voices.

Her first reaction was to flee, to run and hide herself with the knowledge that any intruder, now, would see in an instant what had been going on, but her body was still somnolent; she couldn't move, not quickly enough to escape detection.

But Wyatt could. And before Justine could realise what was happening, he did! There was a fleeting sensation of flight, a single feeling of contact as his fingers gripped her at wrist and ankle, then only the shocking chill of the water as she struck.

She had instinctively gasped as he threw her, and luckily held her breath until her body bobbed to the surface, but in her confusion she couldn't then swim, only gulp and gasp and try to keep herself afloat. There was the vague recollection of a second splash, and suddenly he was there beside her, an arm about her waist as he casually shifted her closer to the shallow end until she found her footing.

'Sorry about that,' he muttered in her ear, and then, 'Hello! Coming to join us, are you?' in casual greeting to the approaching figures of Sebastian and Possum.

'Only if we're not interrupting anything,' Possum replied archly, and Justine felt herself go cold inside. So much for subterfuge, she thought. Wyatt had certainly underestimated his sister's instincts this time.

'Of course you're interrupting,' he replied, to

Justine's surprise. Worse, he made no attempt at all to disguise the hoarseness of his breathing or the electric flickers of barely-subdued passion in his voice. 'If you hadn't interrupted I'd have seduced Justine right there on the apron of the pool.'

She tensed against the grasp of his arm, unsure whether to hit him, try and drown him, or just ignore him. She really wanted only to disappear, vanish like smoke, but she couldn't.

'Oh well, that's all right, then,' Possum replied with a shrug. 'I thought it might be something important, but if that's all . . .' She flung aside her wrap and dived cleanly into the water, emerging squarely in front of them.

Wyatt immediately used his free hand to splash water at her, but the arm around Justine's waist never slackened. 'I would have thought the seduction of Justine was damned well important,' he retorted in mock anger.

'You would, but I reckon Justine's got too much taste to bother with you,' was the casual reply. 'So what *were* you up to?'

'You don't miss much, do you, little sister?' he asked with wry sarcasm, and Justine stifled a giggle at his sheer audacity.

'Not a lot,' Possum replied. 'Now are you going to tell me, or is it to remain a secret for ever?'

'Actually, I'd prefer to have told Justine first,' Wyatt said mysteriously. 'But I suppose it doesn't matter much—I hope not anyway.' He turned to look down into Justine's eyes, his own dark with a glow of hidden satisfaction. 'What I was going to ask, before we were so rudely interrupted,' he said, 'was if you'd mind running the place for me while I trot off to America for three weeks on business?'

'You mean, me . . . run Wyatt's?' She was understandably incredulous, and the look on the faces of Possum and Sebastian revealed their equal surprise.

'That's what I thought I said,' Wyatt replied soberly. 'Have you still got water in your ears or something?'

'No ... but ... well, it just seems a bit much, considering I'm still supposed to be on trial until the end of next week,' Justine replied lamely.

'Oh, that,' he scoffed. 'That was over some time ago. I must have forgotten to tell you.'

Justine stood there, meeting his eyes but unsure herself whether to laugh or cry. Forgotten! If anything, he'd quite deliberately not told her, and wouldn't have now but for this. Still, what was she complaining about? She had the job she wanted ... and very nearly a great deal more in the bargain.

But this! She was suddenly filled with doubts, about her own ability, her rapport with the staff, the likelihood of problems with Gloria, *everything*.

'When ... would I have to take over?' she asked finally, only too aware of his keen scrutiny.

'Tonight.' Succinct and to the point, if nothing else.

'Tonight? But tonight is my turn to be Monday chef!' Possum squealed. 'You can't ...'

'I couldn't think of a better reason,' he interrupted. 'Even the garbage they serve on aeroplanes would be better than what you'd come up with. I'll probably come back to find half my staff down with ptomaine poisoning and the rest on strike in sympathy.'

'Wyatt!' Justine barked the rebuke without thinking, her only concern really for Possum's feelings. She might have saved her breath; Wyatt flinched at the tone, but Possum only shrugged away his charges.

'Too bad for you,' she retorted. 'I'm going to serve duckling à l'orange with julienne potatoes—so there!'

'And mushrooms, too, I'll bet,' he laughed. 'Well, you can give Justine my share; she could do with a few

more pounds.' And gentle fingers pinched lightly at
the curve of Justine's hip, unseen by the others but all
too noticeable to her.

'Oh, can't you go tomorrow? What's one day matter?'
his sister moaned in exaggerated sorrow. 'You never
let me have any fun.'

'I've let you have too damned much; that's the real
trouble,' he replied. 'And this husband of yours, for all
his chauvinistic, foreign ways, is just as bad. You twist
both of us around your little finger.'

'Oh, pooh!'

'And don't pooh me. Why can't you try and be
more like Justine . . . charming and compliant and bid-
dable . . .'

'Like a good dog,' Possum interjected. 'And don't
bother giving us your old line about a good woman
and a good dog both needing a sound thrashing once a
week, either.'

'I've never said any such thing,' he replied hotly,
and obviously lying.

'Hah! You wouldn't dare admit it in front of Justine
anyway,' said Possum. Then she lowered her eyes,
peering up at him cunningly. 'Three weeks, hey? Well,
that should give me time to fill her in on what you're
really like.'

'I'm beginning to think I already know, too well,'
Justine interjected, her own sense of humour coming
to her rescue. 'But you don't have to worry, Possum.
After all, a man with no taste for mushrooms . . .
well . . .'

'Enough!' Wyatt snapped. 'You two can rip me to
shreds when I'm gone, but have the decency to treat
me with due and proper respect to my face, if you
don't mind. Anyway, I've got work to do. Why not
drop by the office later, Justine? Whenever you're
ready . . . there's no panic. But I would like to run
over a few things you'll need to know.'

A moment later he was gone, leaving Justine with a

small, hand-shaped tingling patch on her waist, where he had so casually held her throughout that incredible conversation. Were Possum and Sebastian really so blind that they had totally missed what was happening beneath their very noses? It didn't seem possible, not with Justine's every sense still acutely aware of Wyatt, his touch, his texture, his very being.

She hung about, swimming with them for a few minutes, then made her own excuses and casually—she hoped—strode away towards her own quarters.

It was like moving in a dream. Her mind was already whirling with the implications of being left in charge of Wyatt's, but her body wasn't at all impressed. All that really counted to her physical senses were Wyatt's kisses, his skilful rousing of emotions she had never before believed could be so easily aroused.

Once in the privacy of her suite, she stripped off the wet bikini and stepped into the shower, using alternate bursts of hot and cold water to try and dispel the aching need within her. It was frightening, she thought. No man, and especially not one who was her employer, should have the ability to affect her so.

And to face him, alone again ... that held even greater terrors, because she now realised that Wyatt had only to touch her, even to look at her the right way, whisper her name, and she'd light up again like a petrol bomb.

Still, he'd said there was no hurry. She could leave it, then, until ... after lunch, perhaps. At least that would give her time to straighten herself out, to regain at least a semblance of control.

Once out of the shower she sat herself down at the wide dressing table and began slowly brushing out her hair, seeking comfort and release from her tension in the familiar, monotonous motions. Even as a child, she had found the long process a means to relax, to let her mind blank out problems, but now it seemed to work less well than usual.

The mirrors, those damnable reflections of her every movement! Handy for doing her hair, yet so equally a reminder of everything that had happened that morning. In one, she was able to see exactly the spot where Wyatt's fingers had rubbed ecstasy into the base of her spine; another angle emphasised the long curve of her legs, where his touch had prompted instant, wanton submission.

She closed her eyes, letting her hands continue with the brush. She didn't need to see to brush her hair, definitely didn't need further reminders of Wyatt's incredible touch.

A knock at the door, however, stopped her hand in mid-air. She leapt to her feet, flinging her towelling robe on, and rushed to answer the door with the hairbrush still in her hand.

'Ah, I wondered why you were taking so long,' said the lean, muscular figure in the doorway. And before Justine could think to object, he had walked into the suite and closed the door behind him.

Dressed in snug-fitting casual slacks and a shirt that was open nearly to his waist, Wyatt looked even more devilish than usual, even more under control.

'Here, come and sit down and I'll give you a hand with that,' he said, and Justine placidly obeyed his directions, moving over to sit on a footstool, meekly handing over the hairbrush without a word.

He began to run the brush through her tresses, using long, even strokes that paused only to ensure he didn't pull at the occasional tangle she hadn't yet reached. Then his fingers were quick and deft in their movements, as skilled as those of any professional hairdresser.

'Relaxing, isn't it?' he asked in that particular tone that seeks no answer. 'I should do this more often; it's one way to make sure you'll sit still and listen.'

Then he calmly began to relate the various things Justine would have to take care of during his absence, ticking them off in his mind, she felt, as if he had memorised the list long before.

She listened, absorbed, and didn't have a single question when he had finished talking. And still the brush moved in its metronomic regularity, now starting to crackle little bits of static as the ends of her hair began to dry under his ministrations.

She kept her eyes closed, giving herself to the comfort she had been unable to create, but which this tall, handsome man had somehow started with his first touch on her hair.

Strangely, his touch now was sensual but not sexual. She felt no arousal, no quickening of her passions. Only a gentle lassitude, a rightness, somehow.

Until she opened her eyes and saw the two of them reflected from a dozen angles around her! Then, instantly, she became all too aware of the skimpiness of her robe, of how it was sagging provocatively open at the front, of her legs stretched bare and invitingly out before her.

And of Wyatt's deliberate evaluation of her with the aid of all those damned mirrors! Justine shied like a frightened colt, almost leaping from the footstool as she flinched from his touch. Then somehow she was on her feet, not facing him but speaking from a mouth gone dry and fluttery with alarm.

'I . . . I think you'd better go now,' she stammered, not daring to face him but unable to keep from doing so; his eyes bored into hers via the mirror in front of her.

'Why, I wonder?' he mused, leaning casually to one side long enough to lay down the hairbrush on a side table. 'What are you afraid of, Justine?'

She didn't, couldn't answer. His lean, devilish figure loomed tall above her, his eyes alight with some emotion she didn't dare evaluate.

In a reflection of a reflection of a reflection she saw his hand lift, then felt its intimate touch as he slowly traced one finger down the length of her spine, a touch like living fire even through the material of the robe.

His head dipped and she both saw and felt his lips as they slowly brushed aside the hair to linger on the lobe of her ear, then slide softly, provocatively down the length of her neck. His hands came up to take her by the shoulders, turning her towards him.

'Are you really afraid of me?' he asked in a voice so low she had to strain to hear him, 'or of yourself?'

Then the voice stopped as the lips moved across her cheek, caressing, tantalising as they touched the corner of her mouth, then moved away to slide like velvet over her throat, then back to meet her half-parted lips.

'Please . . . please don't,' she whispered, but it must have been a silent whisper; he gave no sign of hearing. Instead, his hands dropped to close around her waist, pulling her close to him as his lips sought her mouth and closed it with a kiss that was rough and smooth, harsh and gentle, demanding and seducing.

Justine lifted her own arms, fitting against his chest with no force at all as the heat of his body flowed into her finger tips, running like fire up her arms, into her soft, malleable body. Her arms lifted, her fingers tracing light, tentative explorations of their own through the hair on his chest, over the hollows of his collar-bones and then around his neck to gather in the thick hair there.

Without the barrier of her hands, his chest bristled against her; the hair trickled the softness of her half-exposed breasts, tingling against her nipples, rousing them to firm peaks.

Then his hands were there, flicking aside the ties of the robe and bringing their own magic to the fires that now threatened to consume Justine. His touch on her breasts, her stomach, her thighs, seemed like fingers of living fire, lighting answering flames within her as she strained against him, feeling the heat of his body, the hardness of him as she flowed to merge their forms.

'God, but I want you,' his voice whispered, and even as he spoke, strong hands lifted her, gathering her into his arms and cradling her there.

He moved only as far as was necessary, then she felt herself lowered softly on to the great canopied bed.

His lips, his hands, were everywhere then, kissing, caressing, rousing her to a fever that brooked no opposition. When his mouth finally returned to hers, Justine met it eagerly, her fingers frantic as they moved across Wyatt's neck and shoulders, then down across the heat of his chest to touch briefly at his belt.

Then she opened her eyes. Why, she didn't know; perhaps some demon of perversity, perhaps simply the last tiny remnant of common sense within her finally came into being.

And it was enough. When her eyes met the reflection of their tangled bodies in the mirror above, seeing her own nakedness, her shameless reaction to his caresses, something inside rebelled.

'No!' she squealed, suddenly finding strength to thrust at him, wriggling and shoving and pushing with every part of her body as she struggled to free herself. Wyatt, for only a split second, looked bemused. Then, casually despite his surging breath, he lifted himself from the bed and backed away from her.

'All right,' he said softly. 'Relax, Justine . . . it's all right.'

All right! How could anything ever be all right again? Justine's body trembled with the intensity of her revulsion. She flung the robe around her, rolling off the

bed on the side opposite Wyatt, her eyes still wide with
a kind of terror.

'God!' she whispered, then huddled in against herself, arms wrapped across her breasts, head lowered.
'Oh, my God,' she moaned.

'What in hell's the matter?' he demanded suddenly,
starting to reach for her, then thinking better of it and
instead backing away.

The matter? Was the man totally insensitive? And
how could she possibly explain to him the effect of
seeing herself, seeing them ... together, beneath a
brothel mirror? Justine shivered, unable to speak.
There had been something, some aspect of it all, that
had instantly cheapened the whole affair. She didn't
and couldn't deny her own desires, her need of him,
her *wanting*. But not here, not like that!

She couldn't look. She just couldn't! But somehow,
against every feeling inside her, she did. But not at
Wyatt; her glance slid cautiously from beneath lowered
brows to flick upward at the mirror.

'Ah ...' He breathed the comment so softly she
wasn't sure she'd heard it at all, but when he spoke
again, she knew it. Only it didn't make a whole lot of
sense.

'So it should be,' he muttered, almost to himself, it
was so quiet. 'So it should be.'

He turned away, stalking towards the door with a
deliberate stride that to her eyes spelled anger. But
when he turned to look back at her, there was no anger
in his dark eyes, no sign of it on his face. Instead, his
eyes were like pools of black, velvety ink, his face calm
and almost serene.

'You're right, Justine,' he said then. 'I should have
known you would be.'

And he was gone. Not another word, not a gesture
of ... anything. Just gone. Leaving her with only her
conscience, her troubled mind, her trembling, unsatisfied body for company, and, she realised, the in-

disputable knowledge that she was falling ... had fallen ... in love with him.

None of which was the slightest consolation as she wandered the suddenly empty room, oblivious now to the mirrors, oblivious only to what she had somehow given away ... lost ... ended. Being right, she decided, was small consolation.

She thought about it and thought about it and thought about it, and in the end was no wiser.

The remainder of the day dragged by on feet as leaden as her heart, and although Justine had plenty to do, especially with regard to her newly-gained responsibilities, she found it almost impossible to concentrate.

Her accounts suddenly became no more than bewildering jumbles of meaningless figures, the small office in the alcove a claustrophobic cell which threatened to smother her. She even went so far as to try and have an afternoon nap, but her mind refused to accept the numbness of sleep and she quickly abandoned the idea.

Wyatt left without saying goodbye, leaving Justine to wonder if it was by accident or deliberate bloody-mindedness that Gloria was selected to drive him to the airport. That, at least, had one slender consolation; the dark-haired woman's presence was spared them during Possum's debut as a novice chef.

The event was, in Justine's opinion, an unqualified success. Possum's duckling was succulent and tender and served with classic presentation, and her sauce was sufficiently excellent to draw compliments even from Armand, who tended to be even more finicky than Justine herself where sauces were concerned.

Only Wyatt's presence was lacking, and as the evening progressed it seemed that only Justine cared about that. If Possum missed her brother's approval she said nothing, and nobody else seemed to care one way or the other.

Justine let the staff party on somewhat later than usual, justifying it in her own mind because she herself felt no great need for an early night and because they were truly enjoying themselves and obviously having a great time without the shadow of their 'lord and master' hovering over them.

When she finally did go off to bed, however, she vowed to stick to a more rigid discipline in the weeks to come. It wouldn't do at all for Wyatt to find on his return that all of his staff were taking undue advantages of his generosity.

Morning came with a rush. Deliveries, for whatever reason, were earlier than usual and unduly complicated, two of the younger staff members exhibited all-too-obvious hangover symptoms, and Gloria Calder was even more bitchy than usual.

'But Wyatt specifically said that I should take over *all* the accounts,' she complained after flouncing into Justine's office in her usual haughty manner. 'He said you'd be far too busy with everything else to worry about things like that.'

The implication was obvious. Wyatt didn't think Justine was really capable, and was spreading the responsibilities around to make it easy on her. What next, Justine wondered . . . do I get Armand in here telling me I'm not to cook?

'Gloria, I'm sorry, but he didn't tell *me* that,' she argued, only to be immediately interrupted by yet another small crisis, this one involving the wine cellar. Five minutes later she again faced the older woman, but without the desire or strength to argue further.

'Oh, all right. If that's what he said, I guess it's what he wants,' she agreed grudgingly, and handed over her kitchen account books only seconds before Sebastian arrived to advise her of a major booking foul-up.

'I'll take care of everything, Justine. You won't have

to worry about a thing,' Gloria smirked, disappearing with the books and with a self-satisfied, smarmy look on her lovely face.

Ten minutes later another crisis erupted, this one totally unexpected and indeed quite illogical.

'Excuse me, ma'am, but are you Miss Ryan?' asked a well-dressed, businesslike young man who looked round the corner of her alcove as if he expected something to bite him.

'I am,' Justine replied. 'What's your problem?'

'Oh, no problem, really,' he answered. 'It's just that I've come with the drapery material and everything, but I think I need a key. The door's locked, do you see?'

'The door? I'm sorry, but I don't think I know what you mean.'

'To the suite, ma'am. On the third floor.'

Justine shook her head wearily. Could it only be nine-fifteen in the morning?

'You'd better come and show me,' she said, rising from her chair and stretching her neck to dispel a lurking headache pain. What did the man want? Wyatt had said nothing about draperies, much less about anything for the third floor. Or had he? Justine racked her brain, but couldn't recall anything.

She led the man up the private staircase, fingers jingling the massive key-ring that gave her access to the various storage areas of the house, Wyatt's personal suite, her own suite, and the guest rooms, pool enclosure and garages.

'It's this one, according to the diagram I have,' the man said, and Justine stood silent with disbelief. Her own suite! But it couldn't be.

'Are you sure?' she asked. 'You *did* get your instructions from Mr Burns, I gather?'

'Oh yes. Yesterday afternoon,' he replied, holding up a diagram in Wyatt's unmistakable handwriting. 'And it's very definitely this one, see? He said there were all kinds of mirrors that he wanted covered over.'

Justine could have fallen through the floor. Her brain reeled, but it was her heart that was most stricken by the man's words. Mirrors covered? In *her* suite? The implications were only too obvious.

'I think you'd best explain to me just exactly what your instructions were,' she said as they stepped into the room.

'Oh, just to arrange draperies to cover up the . . . My God!' exclaimed the man, halting to stare incredulously around the room. 'What did they keep in here . . . a harem?'

'Something like that,' Justine replied drily, then swallowed the enormous lump that had suddenly emerged in her throat. 'It's . . . a very historic room, I'm told.'

'Historic isn't the word for it,' commented the draper. 'This is a real passion-pit, this is. Look at that bed, would you? Lord love us, but I can see why he wants the place curtained off; it's enough to give a monk ideas!'

And I'm no monk, Justine thought, suddenly seeing the suite as if for the first time. Whatever had prompted her to accept this accommodation, she wondered, and more important, what had ever prompted Wyatt to insist on it?

A quick glance assured her that her more personal, private possessions were safely put away, and whatever this decorator might find in his measuring could hardly matter.

'Look,' she said, 'I'm really very busy here today, so is it all right if I leave you now, and I'll come and lock up again when you're done?'

He turned to look at her, eyes dazed with a masculine fantasy she didn't really want to comprehend. 'Oh . . . oh, all right,' he muttered, already turning away. 'I won't be more than, say, an hour or so.'

'Right! Just let me know, then,' she said, and quickly fled before his fantasies got out of hand. Damn Wyatt Burns anyway, she thought. And damn Justine Ryan, too, for ever allowing herself to get mixed up in this mess.

But as she returned to her myriad duties, there was a tiny, embryonic glow of pleasure inside her. Wyatt had, without question, thought enough of her feelings to make this effort. Surely, she thought, that must count for something? But what?

Justine found out *what* only twenty-four hours later, when the decorator returned to once again seek the key to her suite, spent most of the day trotting back and forth with armfuls of fabric, and finally demanded her presence—as Wyatt's deputy—for a final approval.

The effect was magnificent! Without in any way permanently destroying the historic significance of the suite—although Justine was tempted to question that significance on general principles—the decorator had resolved the – mirror problem with a truly talented display of hanging draperies that covered the mirrors if desired, but could be drawn open to return the suite to its original decadent opulence. Even the massive, betraying mirror above the bed had been covered in heavy soft fabric.

'Excellent,' she declared. 'I'm sure Mr Burns will be really pleased.' And she sent the little man on his way so that she could revel in the new-found luxury of her quarters.

It was indeed thoughtful of Wyatt, she thought, although not without a twinge of concern about the obvious cost. She still hadn't quite figured out his logic in redecorating the room; did he plan a replay of their last encounter? If so, even the draperies couldn't obscure her instinctive fear of such a happening, and Justine vowed to have a third party present when she showed him the result of his order, and indeed vowed

further never to let herself be caught alone with him in
this room again, curtains or no curtains.

But there was a certain satisfaction about allowing
those invoices to go directly to Gloria. What would the
attractive brunette think of them? she wondered. And
immediately chastised herself for being bitchy. To let
herself drop down to Gloria's level was unthinkable,
but oh, so tempting.

The few days following were a delight, although a
harassed, overworked delight, Justine found. She was
literally everywhere in the building, supervising not
only her kitchens but other aspects of the restaurant
that had earlier been quite remote from her own
work.

Possum was a great help. The girl who showed
incredible acting talent before her husband and
brother was, Justine found, a person of incredible,
down-to-earth practicality. Through her exposure at
Wyatt's and her husband's Greek establishment, she
had a mammoth knowledge of exactly how restaurants
were operated, and she freely shared it with Justine.

But it was on Justine's shoulders that the major
workload fell, and when Wyatt had been gone a week
and a day, Justine was more than prepared to grant
him an endurance she couldn't personally match.

One night had seen a visitation by that same, horrid
restaurant columnist who had discussed her in less-
than-endearing terms in the kitchen of her last place of
employment, and Justine had been thankful to find him
so obviously attracted to Gloria that he seemed to—
quite ignore her own presence.

By the end of the first week, she had begun to find a
rhythm to it all, and was genuinely revelling in the
smooth operation of both kitchen and overall restaurant. Even Gloria, for whatever reason, seemed to
have settled into Justine's operational pattern.

But Possum was bored, and made no bones about
expressing her boredom when the two girls shared an

impromptu lunch on the Monday after Wyatt's departure.

'Why do we have to stick to this traditional Ye Olde English tucker?' Possum moaned. 'I know it fits the decor and everything, but Sebastian says a growing number of customers are asking for dishes we simply don't offer. Damn Wyatt anyway! It's only his stubbornness that keeps us from being a really international restaurant.'

The next day, Justine found herself in total agreement, having just lost a booking for twenty because of the restricted menu. The potential client had wanted a mixed, international menu for his group, and through Wyatt's restrictions Justine had been forced to pass on the booking.

'Not impressive,' she muttered as she hung up the telephone. 'Not impressive at all. I wonder . . .'

Two days later she had it under control. The smallest of the original 'swinging London' rooms had been transformed into an 'international room', with a daily-changing menu that sprawled across Europe, Asia and Indonesia, offering a different country's menu each day.

'I don't think your brother's going to approve at all, unless we can prove the economics of it all,' Justine told Possum. But within three days of the changeover, it became obvious her instincts had been right after all. People flooded the new section, ordering not off the menu, but simply asking for the chef's specials of the day and obviously enjoying them.

The economics were proved within that three-day period; bookings doubled and then tripled as the word spread that Wyatt's was no longer bound to Ye Olde English tradition.

'You're set for life,' Possum decreed. But Justine wasn't all that easily convinced. True, the experiment had been a rousing success. But she had had at least one complaint from a Colonel Blimp type about a lowering of standards, and she fully expected Wyatt to follow it up.

But how could he *really* object, considering the overall success? Justine couldn't see it, yet she had a deep-seated feeling that Wyatt's return might be even more traumatic than his departure.

A thoroughly supportive view expressed by *that* restaurant columnist, who had obviously returned to check on the changeover, didn't do a lot for Justine's feeling that she had stepped beyond the pale. Certainly Wyatt couldn't dispute the plaudits in the column, and yet . . .

The always imperative telephone interrupted Justine's thoughts, and she picked up the receiver to hear an unexpected yet familiar voice.

'Well, aren't you the one? And to think you never even considered the feelings of an old friend.'

'Adrienne Charles! But what are you on about?' Justine replied with a mixture of surprise and delight.

'On about? Well, that perfectly ridiculous column of good old whatshisname's yesterday, what else?' was the caustic reply. 'I mean, really, Justine! To give that gross, porcine fellow first dibs at the new Wyatt's and leave my very civilised magazine out in the cold. You should have your head examined!'

'Whatever are you on about?' Justine asked again, totally confused by the notes of friendship and cold business in her old school chum's voice.

'Oh, but of course, you couldn't know,' Adrienne cooed. Then she simpered on about her latest job with a high-quality gourmet magazine and the fact that she just *must* have an interview with Justine for the next month's issue.

'Oh, I don't think so,' Justine hedged. 'I think you'd better wait until Wyatt . . . Mr Burns . . . gets back. It's only a matter of a week and a bit . . .'

'Nonsense! I have deadlines and you have the in-

credible fortune to know the top restaurant writer in
the business,' said Adrienne, ignoring completely the
fact that Justine hadn't even known about her job, and
would have, were it as important as she let on.

'I'll be there for lunch tomorrow, photographer and
all,' Adrienne went on. 'Nothing fancy, of course, but
enough to give me adequate copy about your excellent
continental cuisine. Everyone . . . and I mean *everyone*
is raving about it, so I'm sure I'll be able to create a
veritable gem of an article.'

'Yes . . . but . . . but what about Wyatt . . . Mr
Burns?' Justine asked yet again. Too late; her friend
had already rung off, leaving Justine with more than a
few qualms about what was to come. She knew
Adrienne only too well, and having not heard one word
about Adrienne's entry into the select world of metro-
politan restaurant columnists, she held immediate sus-
picions about what her old school friend might be
trying on.

Sure enough! When Adrienne arrived next day with
a scruffy, greasy-haired photographer in tow, it was to
first admit that she didn't really work for the magazine
in question, but had gained herself a freelance entrée
into a possible future job.

'You've just got to help me, Justine,' she pleaded
openly. 'If I can just swing the editor round to considering this life-style series—and I *can*, with Wyatt's
as the first instalment—than I'm set for a job, no
worries. Please, Justine!'

It took Justine back to her schooldays, but she forced
from her mind the inevitable results of an Adrienne
plea and gave in, though not without a twinge of mis-
giving. She watched her friend dabble at a luxurious
lunch, while the young photographer gobbled his food
eagerly, and dutifully answered the questions as they
came.

'Right,' Adrienne said finally, reaching down to
replace notebook and pen in her copious handbag.

'Now, Justine, tell me what Wyatt Burns is *really* like.'

'I don't think there's much I can tell you,' said Justine, visibly relaxing now that the interview was over. 'He's very organised, very professional . . .'

'And very handsome, with a womanising reputation to match,' Adrianne interrupted. 'Come on, don't you fancy him just a little?'

'Certainly not!' Justine lied, quite convincingly, she thought. 'He's also rude, domineering, overbearing, and extremely chauvinistic. I think he'd have women chained in the kitchen for life if he had his way.'

'Hah! More like the bedroom, if you ask me.'

'Well, it's the same thing,' Justine countered. 'He's the most arrogant, chauvinistic man I've ever met; he makes the worst of the Parisians I know seem like yappy little puppydogs. I'm not kidding, Adrienne. I still don't know what I'm doing here; he damned near sacked me the moment he saw me—didn't want a female chef here for anything.'

Adrienne arched one daintily-plucked eyebrow. 'But you're still here, and managing the place in his absence, no less. You must have done a mighty job of changing his mind.'

'Humph! Nobody changed Wyatt's mind but Wyatt,' Justine snorted. 'He'll likely have my head on a platter for this international menu idea, despite its popularity.'

'Oh, surely not! He'd be too good a businessman for that,' Adrienne replied, but Justine was hardly listening as she watched the grotty little photographer scuttling around with his cameras in action.

'How about in the kitchen? Does he interfere with your work very much?' Adrianne continued.

'Oh . . . oh, no,' was the reply. 'I hardly ever see him in the kitchen, which is just as well,' said Justine. 'And if he did get in the way I'd only have to start cooking mushrooms and he'd be gone in a flash. He cannot *abide* mushrooms.'

'Interesting. Well, anyway, dear, I must be off now. I see we've got all the pix we'll need.'

'All right. But please, Adrienne, don't make too much of that interview, will you? I don't want all kinds of trouble with Wyatt when he comes back.'

'Of course not,' Adrienne assured her. 'As I said, I'm not even sure I can sell it, and in any event it would be ages before it's published. You know how the magazine business works . . . they're always several months ahead.'

Justine didn't, and indeed she was already having very strong second thoughts. 'Well, just remember that *my* job's at stake in this too,' she cautioned. 'I know you want to make a good impression, but . . .'

'Not to worry,' was the quick reply.

So Justine didn't—not until the day Wyatt returned. And by then it was far, far too late to worry.

CHAPTER SIX

SHE was at her desk, without the slightest idea that he had returned, and the voice that rumbled through the intercom was the growl of some fearsome, angry beast.

'Justine! Get yourself up here to my office. Now!'

No time to wonder, to question, even to reply. The decisive click of the intercom going off was as unfeelingly mechanical as the voice itself.

And when she knocked tentatively on the door of Wyatt's office, the barked demand for her presence inside was more than enough warning that something was very, very wrong.

Wyatt's face was a thundercloud, eyes snapping like bolts of lightning as he watched Justine enter and walk uneasily towards his desk. He brusquely gestured for her to be seated, but before her bottom touched the chair she was reaching to catch the folded magazine he had flung at her.

'Just what the bloody hell is this?' he demanded through gritted teeth, and she could feel him struggling for control.

Adrienne! The thought scorched through her like a brand even as she looked at the story. Then Justine's eyes widened and she began to tremble, only not through fear, but vivid, righteous, all-encompassing rage.

'The bitch!' she cried. 'Oh, but ... I ... I didn't ...' She couldn't go on. Anger and sheer outrage had ensnared her tongue and her mind as well.

'You *didn't*? Well then, just who the hell is that in the picture, the blonde one with the big mouth?' he sneered. 'The one with the employer who's rude, domineering, overbearing and extremely chauvinistic?

Who'd have women chained up in the kitchen if he had his way? The one who bloody well *will* have your head on a platter, you judas bitch!'

'But . . . but I didn't,' Justine protested. 'She'd put away her . . . notebook . . .' And, she realised upon reading her own exact words, replaced it with a hidden tape recorder. It was all there—every single word of their supposedly off-the-record chat. Even the comment about the mushrooms.

She fell silent and stayed that way. What could she possibly say, even if she were able to speak around the giant knot in her stomach?

The article was everything he thought it was, a total, complete betrayal, a startling breach of confidence not only to her, but *by* her. The fact that her old school *friend* had brazenly led her down the garden path and callously dumped her in the proverbial compost bin was nothing when compared to the damage it all must have done to Wyatt's personal image. No wonder he was so angry!

She would have cried, only she was too numbed by the whole thing for crying . . . yet. In fact her unwanted, unthinking reaction was to laugh hysterically.

'And I suppose you *didn't* allow the photographer to take those pictures,' Wyatt's accusing growl continued. 'And you *didn't* blatantly ignore my opinions when you created this international section in the menu. Tell me, Justine, just what the hell *did* you do? Take complete and utter leave of your senses? That's obvious,' he continued without waiting for any form of reply. 'But what I don't understand is why. Surely you can't have been that annoyed with me, and I just can't believe you'd normally be that deceitful, that damnably underhanded.'

'I . . . I wasn't . . .' she tried to say, only to have him roar across her timorous voice.

'Damn it, can't you talk either? Surely you must

have had some reason for trying to completely discredit this house and everything it stands for.'

'I didn't . . . I didn't!' she cried. And then, suddenly angry for all her despair: 'I increased our turnover by an average twenty-four per cent with my international menu, but still, I only did it as an experiment. Possum and I thought . . .'

'Possum? Bloody hell, woman, surely you haven't been listening to my scatterbrained sister? Hell!' And he slammed the desk so angrily with his fist that pens and pencils danced in fear before cowering silent again.

'Damn you!' Justine screamed out her fear in pure defence. 'Didn't you listen? A twenty-four per cent increase in turnover. Twenty-four per cent! Doesn't that count for anything?'

'Not when you do it without my permission!' He, too, seemed to be shouting now, his voice like thunder in the room.

'Your permission! What am I, your slave?' she retorted. Now her anger was becoming more real than defensive. 'Well, you know where you can stick that idea, *Mr* Wyatt Burns! With mushrooms, and I hope you choke. I'm a professional and you hired me as a professional, and any sensible man would damned well appreciate my little experiment for its success!'

'And ignore the complaints as being purely irrelevant, I suppose,' he sneered, upper lip curled back to reveal teeth that seemed to Justine like those of a ravening wolf.

'What complaints? Show me the complaints,' she raged, no longer totally in control. She lunged to her feet, her own palm now slamming into the top of the desk as she leaned across it and hissed at him like an angry alleycat.

Wordless, he reached to a small stack of papers on his desk and flung them down like a gauntlet before her. Justine snatched them up, half her mind relieved that there were so few, the rest apprehensive about the contents.

It took her only an instant, it seemed, to scan them. One was obviously from the Colonel Blimp type; two more were from unquestionable supporters who she doubted had ever been inside Wyatt's, and a final one was from somebody who didn't think the Italian dish they had been served was really genuine.

'My God! And you want to sack me for this load of rubbish?' she cried angrily. 'Well, go ahead . . . just go ahead. In fact, don't even bother. I quit! If this is any example of the way you treat your chefs I can do without you *and* your restaurant!'

She was already half turned away when an iron hand clamped on to her wrist, pinning her to the desk like a butterfly in a display case.

'Who said anything about sacking you?' Wyatt asked in a voice gone suddenly, frighteningly, deceptively quiet. 'Not that I shouldn't, mind, after that damned interview.'

'Oh, bother the interview!' Justine snapped. 'If you'd so much as bothered to ask, I'd have told you it was as much of a surprise to me as it was to you. Damn Adrienne, anyway; the bitch used to be my friend, if you can imagine it. But I *did* not, and *would* not, discuss things like she's printed as part of any interview, and you should know that, too. I just wouldn't! Oh, wait until I get my hands on her . . . I'll . . .'

'You'll what?' he asked, interrupting her before she could even think of a suitable punishment. 'And do you honestly mean to tell me that what she's printed here wasn't part of the interview?'

'Damn it! Isn't that what I've just been saying?' she raged, oblivious to the tears that now streaked down unnoticed across her pale cheeks. 'She'd already put away her notebook and I thought we were just . . . chatting like old friends. Friends! Oh, my heavens . . .'

'Friends like that and you don't need any enemies,' he growled. 'Funny, I seem to have employees like that . . .'

'You do not! What I said to her was . . . supposed to be confidential,' Justine replied.

'But true.' Wyatt's voice was once again soft, but his eyes were anything but! They seemed to glow at her like coals, threatening, lurking, menacing.

She didn't reply. What sense to it? The words, when said, had seemed true enough if somewhat exaggerated for effect. But reading them? In print the truth seemed totally overshadowed by the effect. Even the remark about him not liking mushrooms seemed an accusation. He had every right to be angry.

'I'm only surprised there's nothing in the story about my making a pass at you . . . or didn't she bother to ask about that?' he said then.

'She . . . tried,' Justine replied lamely. How sense-less, now, to try and tell him how private that was to her, how sensitive, how . . . intimate. It would only make her look even more of a fool.

'Obviously not very hard . . . or were you just pro-tecting your own reputation?' he sneered. 'Didn't you take her up for a woman's-eye view of the brothel? That would have made marvellous copy, wouldn't it— Restaurateur keeps Chef in Mirrored Love Nest!'

Justine gasped at the cruelty of it, but Wyatt ignored her pain.

'I think you'd better trot off down and chain yourself up again in your kitchen,' he said coldly. 'Obviously you were too busy making sweeping changes and giving ridiculous interviews to get the books up to date, and I'd like a clearer picture of what's really happening before I decide what to do about you.'

'But the books are up to date,' Justine replied, now totally confused. 'At least, they were up to yesterday. I haven't got round to them yet today.'

'If that's what you call book-keeping, thank heaven

you're a chef,' he retorted angrily. 'Now get yourself out of here and see if you can manage to spend some time doing what you're paid to do!'

She left, stunned by the stolid coldness of his attitude. In the kitchen, Armand was busy with the initial preparations on that day's international special, and Justine didn't know whether to stop him or let him continue. It seemed most likely that Wyatt would quickly put an end to her experiment, but there were half a dozen bookings for that evening made especially because of the international special, and she didn't quite dare cancel at this stage.

Let him cancel if he wants to, she thought, and let *him* explain it to the customers, while he's at it.

Instead she busied herself by checking the various meats in the enormous cold room, and it wasn't until she had been there almost ten minutes that she had calmed down sufficiently to risk speaking to anyone.

Cooled down is right, she thought idly, inspecting the goosebumps on her forearms as she reached for the inside latch. She usually would have put on a sweater or coverall before making such an intensive assessment.

Justine pushed at the latch, then cursed under her breath when it refused to move. Damn the thing! She pushed again, and yet again, but something was obviously wrong. The latch simply wouldn't move.

She kicked at the door in her anger, realising the sound wouldn't carry through the heavy, insulated walls, and was about to kick again when the door suddenly opened.

'I did not realise you were here,' said Armand, his arms full of packaged meats. 'The butcher he has come and gone, but as I could not find you . . .'

'It doesn't matter, Armand,' Justine replied, interrupting him. She was in no mood at this moment to engage in small talk with her own butcher or suffer the pig-eyed leers of the oaf she had sacked and Wyatt had reinstated.

'Listen, we must check the latch on this cold room,' she explained. 'It's . . . sticking or something. I almost got locked in there.'

He looked perturbed. 'It was all right only a half an hour ago,' he said. 'I will check it now, however.'

He stepped into the cold room, slamming the heavy door after him. Justine stood uncertainly on the outside, but an instant later the door swung open without her help, then closed and opened three more times.

'It seems fine to me,' said Armand, emerging empty-handed. 'And in any case we cannot have it checked now until Monday, unless you wish to pay a horrible overtime bill for it. But I think it is all right.'

Justine glanced at her wrist-watch. One-thirty! This was one Saturday, she decided, that had already got off to a bad start; she'd completely lost the morning.

'Well, we'll have to be careful with it, just in case,' she replied. 'Please let everybody know that it's suspect, so they don't go wandering in there without somebody knowing about it.'

'I will do that,' he replied gravely, and Justine turned away, only to stop just short of walking straight through Gloria Calder.

'I'm sorry, Gloria,' she said with a sad shake of her head. 'What can I do for you?'

Gloria stood there silently, her eyes watchful until Armand had walked away. When she finally spoke it wasn't until she was quite sure they wouldn't be overheard.

'I think you've already done it,' she said then, with a malicious gleam in her eyes. 'I just came to say thank you and ask if you've a new job lined up.'

Justine went cold inside, colder than she had even thought of being while inside the cool room. So that was the way of it, she thought. Not only sacked, but having to hear it from . . . No, not from Gloria . . . if

Wyatt was to sack her he would damned well have to do it himself. In person.

Keeping a calm exterior despite the sick feeling inside, she contrived to smile sweetly as she replied.

'Why, thank you, Gloria. But I think you might be just a little ahead of yourself,' she replied, and quickly turned and walked away without any attempt at explanation. If she was already sacked, none would be needed, and if she wasn't . . . well, she'd worry about it later. It was none of Gloria's business in any event.

None of which was the slightest consolation as she plunged into the arduous task of preparing for that evening's diners. One of the juniors was ill, bookings were right to the maximum and it would be a hard night's slogging for all concerned.

Justine's own troubled conscience and her growing certainty that a sacking was inevitable made her a vicious taskmistress throughout the afternoon, even though she recognised the problem and did her level best to maintain an even temper.

Wyatt, fortunately, avoided the kitchen entirely. Had he interrupted her delicate tightrope of control, Justine was certain she wouldn't have had to be sacked—she'd have quit out of hand.

As it was, only Sebastian and the unflappable actress Possum managed to avoid her foul temper and changeable temperament. Sebastian merely stayed out of the kitchen, while Possum, for perhaps the first time since Justine's arrival at Wyatt's, behaved impeccably.

When Wyatt finally did make an appearance, it was midway through the evening. He was, as might be expected in his position as host, impeccably dressed and groomed, but what surprised Justine was not his appearance but his attitude.

'How are you coping in here?' he asked quite pleasantly. 'I don't suppose you've a moment to step into your international corner with me?'

'I . . . could,' Justine replied cautiously, then looked

at her no-longer-immaculate coverall. 'But I really
don't think . . . I mean, look at me.'

'So take two minutes and change into a clean outfit,'
he replied evenly. 'You do have one, I presume?'

'Well, of course,' she replied, biting back the sting
in the words, but only too aware of how one dark eyebrow
raised almost as a caution against further insolence.

'Right, I'll see you out there,' he replied, and was
gone, with only the most casual of glances at what the
rest of the busy staff were doing.

'I don't need this,' Justine muttered to herself as she
swiftly exchanged the coverall for a shiny, whiter-than-
white one. 'I don't need this at all.'

But she finally went, as of course she had to, and
once through the swinging doors into the restaurant
proper she threw back her shoulders and advanced
upon the table where Wyatt was sitting with as much
dignity as she could muster.

With him at the table were three other men, one of
them quite elderly and the others in their late thirties.
All four men rose politely as Justine approached. Her
mind was so occupied trying to relate table number to
a suddenly vanished mental bookings list that she could
only nod when Wyatt smiled and took her hand.

'This, gentlemen, is the genius behind Wyatt's successful international corner,' he said with a wide grin.
'May I present Miss Justine Ryan, *chef extraordinaire*,
to whom must go *all* credit for it. But please don't try
to hire her away, because I've got her on a very long-
term contract.'

He introduced the men, but their names floated away
in the haze of Justine's confusion. All she did understand was that they were involved together in a chain
of quality restaurants developed in Melbourne, and
that they were in the process of seeking expansion
properties in Sydney.

'You've time for a glass of wine, Justine,' Wyatt said
in tones that brooked no possible objection. He had

only to nod and it was there before her, complete with a broad wink from Possum, who brought it.

'I must certainly congratulate you, Miss Ryan,' said the elder of three men. 'Your international corner concept has been developed with the best of taste and all else that matters. The only thing that does surprise me is that you chose to instigate the move while Wyatt was off in America.' And the look in his eye said more than his words.

The look in Wyatt's eyes said even more, and Justine took a slow breath and thought very quickly indeed before answering. 'Well, of course we'd discussed it before he left,' she said then, struggling to keep a straight face.

'Indeed? I thought it must be so,' replied her inquisitor, only to be replaced by one of his younger companions.

'I'll bet you didn't discuss that interview you gave Adrienne Charles,' he chuckled. 'Now *that* was a stroke of genius, not that I want to take anything away from your international concept.'

Genius! A stroke of sheer idiocy, bad luck, bad management and outright stupidity, Justine thought. But genius? Not much!

Obviously, however, she wasn't expected to reply to the somewhat ludicrous compliment. The man continued without waiting for any answer.

'It's done wonders for Wyatt's image, although I'm damned sure he won't admit it,' he said. 'Just imagine a restaurateur who doesn't like mushrooms . . . the whole thing has humanised him beyond belief. Not that we could expect him to honestly say he appreciated being termed a male chauvinist pig—which he is and always has been—but he forgets that the public thrives on that sort of drivel. I'll bet your bookings have increased noticeably since that column came out, eh, Wyatt?'

'As if I'd tell you,' was the laconic reply. 'And I

am not a male chauvinist pig . . . only a piglet at best. Justine may yet pay for her part in that interview.'

'Pay? You should give her a bonus,' cut in the older of the three men. 'And another one for what she's done here.' He turned to Justine with a broad smile. 'And see that he does, my dear. If not, break your contract and come and work for me. I mean that.' And as if in proof, he placed his business card in Justine's hand and gave Wyatt a hard look.

'Unfair . . . unfair!' Wyatt protested. 'I haven't even been back a full day and already you're trying to steal my staff.'

'All part of business, old friend,' laughed the older man. 'If you haven't the good sense to appreciate your staff, you must expect those of us who are more experienced to take full advantage.'

'If anybody's going to take advantage of Justine, it will be me,' Wyatt replied suggestively and his eyes locked with hers as if defying her to object. 'I have a great deal of appreciation for Justine, and well she knows it.'

'You'd have to be a fool not to,' responded the third of the men, who up to that moment had said nothing. He was a tall, well set up young man with auburn hair and deep-set blue eyes that had already assessed Justine's figure quite thoroughly during the conversation. Not as tall as Wyatt, he was more conventionally handsome, almost pretty.

More significant, his interest in Justine had little to do with her cooking abilities; that was obvious both to her and to Wyatt, who shot the other man an eyebrow-raised glance and then grinned wolfishly.

But he said nothing, and Justine claimed that moment of relative silence to make her own bid for escape.

'Thank you *all* for the pretty compliments. And the wine, of course,' she said. 'But now I really must retire to my cauldrons.'

She started to rise, but was halted by a gesture from Wyatt. 'Five minutes won't make any difference,' he said. 'Have another glass of wine and then we'll let you go back to feeding the multitudes.'

'Is that an order?' she asked, looking at him sideways in a gesture that could have been coquettish but wasn't really intended that way.

'It is! Peter hasn't finished admiring you, and I wouldn't want him to leave Wyatt's unsatisfied since he is, after all, a guest here.'

'You'd better find yourself a standby cook, then,' grinned the auburn-haired man. 'Because with all due respect to the chef, I find Justine more than lives up to her reputation.'

What reputation? she wondered, but couldn't quite summon the nerve to meet Wyatt's dark eyes as he laughed harshly at the compliment.

Then, having ordered her so directly to stay, he turned his attentions to a distinctly business discussion with the older of the three men, leaving Justine to the mercies of Peter's attention.

He was, Justine decided in an instant, a womaniser of the highest order. Smooth, sauve, charming . . . and really very attractive. But not really her type.

Nonetheless, when his subtle questioning revealed that she wouldn't be working the next day, she quite agreeably accepted his invitation to go for a drive and have lunch somewhere.

'I'll let you choose where,' he said with a smile. 'Just so long as it isn't anywhere I'd want to get financially involved. When I'm lunching with a beautiful woman I don't want to be distracted by anything as vulgar as money.'

'I think you flatter me far too much,' she replied, a bit tongue in cheek, 'but I'll certainly see that I keep your requirements in mind.'

'I'm sure you will,' Peter replied, and would have said more, Justine thought, except that her own atten-

tion was diverted by Possum standing off to one side
making panic signals.

'Look, I'm sorry, but I *must* run,' Justine apologised,
and was on her way to the kitchen in seconds. The
panic, thank goodness, was a relatively minor one, but
she didn't return to the international corner, and
wasn't at all surprised when there was no further
demand for her presence.

It wasn't until everything was wrapped up for the
evening and she was alone in her suite that Justine had
a moment to seriously consider the implications of her
accepting Peter's invitation.

To provoke Wyatt? No, she thought, and immediately chuckled at the blatancy of the lie.

'Of course you tried to provoke Wyatt, you silly
woman,' she muttered at herself in the bathroom
mirror. 'And didn't you just make a thorough mess of
it, too? He didn't notice—couldn't have cared less, in
fact—and now you're stuck with a date you don't really
want or need.'

Although even that, she admitted later, wasn't totally
true. Peter . . . Grice, that was it . . . was a pleasant
and very charming man. Certainly not a man who
would have difficulty finding feminine company,
which made his invitation flattering if nothing else. But
he wasn't her type. Her type! He wasn't Wyatt, that
was the essence of it.

Justine had almost talked herself into a last-minute
excuse when Peter arrived the next morning, but at
that same last minute she decided instead to go out
with him. There had been neither sight nor sound of
Wyatt, not that she should have expected any, she
supposed, so she had absolutely no excuse for changing
her mind.

They drove south first, for a leisurely visit to the
Royal National Park and its splendid vistas of ocean,
beach and thick scrub forest. Throughout the drive in
his powerful rented car, Peter kept Justine amused and

usually laughing happily with his outrageous tales of restaurants he had known and the people involved in them. He was well travelled and knowledgeable, but most important, he was simply good fun to be with.

There was, somewhat to Justine's surprise at first, simply no sexual tension between them. Peter obviously found her attractive and he seemed to be enjoying her company as much as she enjoyed his, but there was none of the innuendo and games-playing she would have expected.

She understood much better when they finally settled down for lunch at a place Justine had selected for its classic French cuisine. Peter, somewhat hesitantly, she thought, brought out a picture of a petite, almost delicate blonde girl—and the announcement that he was planning to ask her to marry him when he got back to Melbourne.

'I would have done it before, but Sue's a Sydney girl at heart, and I wanted to be sure of this expansion programme first,' he explained, adding that he would be the partnership representative selected to shift bases to Sydney to oversee the operation.

Then, as if in reply to her unspoken question about why he should have chosen to ask her out, he chuckled quite diabolically and continued.

'Don't be offended, but I really did have a kind of devilish urge last night to see if I couldn't get old Wyatt stirred up a bit. And I did take an immediate liking to you as well.'

He swallowed and for an instant looked quite perplexed. 'Damn, that sounded terribly condescending, didn't it? Maybe if I try it the other way round. I was very definitely drawn to you, although not in perhaps the most classic way, and when I saw Wyatt might be vulnerable, I . . . oh . . . wrong again.'

Justine could have choked herself from the laughter inside, and she took pity on him immediately.

'Look, I do understand . . . well, sort of,' she

replied. 'And truly I've enjoyed myself quite as much today as I think you have, Peter, so stop making matters worse with these apology attempts.'

Privately, she suspected he had had just a touch too much wine the evening before, and could find no honourable escape when faced with his assignation attempt. But she also very much believed his assertion about stirring Wyatt, since she already knew that Peter had worked for Wyatt some years before and the two were fast friends of long standing.

She laughed, then. 'I think you really misjudged part of the situation, though. About stirring Wyatt, I mean. And just as well, too, since there's nothing between us and I can't say I'd want there to be.'

Then it was Peter's turn to laugh, and he did so with great gusto now that their little misunderstanding was cleared up without hard feelings.

'You'd better look again, lady,' he told her. 'I've known Wyatt too long not to be able to read him just a little bit, and he's interested all right. As for you, may I simply say that there's an old quote about ladies protesting too much.'

'Well then, I'll protest even more,' she retorted, hoping her sudden lift in spirit didn't show all over her face. So Wyatt was interested? He'd a funny way of showing it, she thought, unless Peter's definition of interested involved purely sexual implications. But how could she ask?

She couldn't, of course, and Peter let that aspect of their conversation drop when the first course arrived. Instead, they talked throughout the meal about his ideas for the group's restaurant chain, and about Justine's own ideas for the small restaurant she might some day own herself.

'Sebastian and Possum have the right idea, I think,' she said at one point. 'They're both working terribly hard to get the place·off the ground, but they're succeeding. And when it's all under control they'll be in for a great deal of satisfaction.'

'Fine, but how about money? Or isn't that important to them?' Peter was interested, but restaurants to him had a different significance than Justine imagined existed for Sebastian and Possum.

'Oh, I think they'll make enough,' she said. 'But for them I honestly think the satisfaction will be the real incentive. Possum dearly wants to be a proper chef, and despite Wyatt's opinion I think she'll make it.'

Peter laughed. 'Well, there's no doubt that Sebastian will make it. He's got to be the biggest ham this side of creation. In fact, why don't we get together tonight and pay their place a visit? I'd love to see him do his Zorba routine, having already been quite taken in by the British butler act last night.'

'All right,' said Justine. 'It's time I paid them another visit anyway. Only tonight I'll drive myself, if you don't mind. It's ludicrous for you to be travelling that sort of distances for me under the circumstances.'

'Ouch! That was a low blow,' he replied. 'And I would do it gladly; I want you to know that.'

'I wouldn't have offered if I didn't know,' she smiled. And then with a little grin of friendly mischief: 'I just hope your fiancée appreciates me for my restraint, that's all.'

'Hah! Strike two for Justine,' Peter laughed. 'I'll ask her when I phone this afternoon and let you know at dinner. I'll even leave it to you to make a booking, so there!'

When he finally dropped her back at Wyatt's it was nearly three o'clock, so they agreed that a later dinner would be best.

'I'll meet you there at eight-thirty,' said Justine, 'and don't be late, either. That's purely a feminine prerogative and although I seldom use it, I'd like to keep it feminine just in case.'

She herself had no intention of being late. She spent the remainder of the afternoon swimming and resting, then devoted a full hour to her hair, clothes and make-up. She already knew that while Possum would be performing that evening, there would also be ample opportunity for the patrons to dance and it would seem ludicrous not to expect Peter to become involved in that.

During Wyatt's American visit, Justine had devoted a portion of her income to some going-out type clothes, her favourite of which was a flowing, caftan-styled dress in a delicate mauve colour that suited her colouring perfectly.

Wyatt, she thought idly, would probably quite like the dress. It depended for its effect more on cut and material than brazen display of what was beneath, but as she swirled before the mirror, hair piled high and pinned just sufficiently to hold it there, the dress was magnificent.

She wanted to be a bit early at the restaurant, so it was only seven-thirty when she descended the rear staircase and strolled over to manipulate her small car from the restaurant garage. She had just backed out of the building, and was about to leave the car to close the garage doors when a shadowy figure stepped forward to hold up a commanding palm.

'Don't bother; I'll get the doors for you,' said Wyatt, looking his usual elegant self in a dark blue dinner jacket over a gleaming ruffled shirt and dark trousers.

He paused beside the small car and stooped to peer in at her, his eyes lingering as they roved over what he could see of her dress and hair.

'Impressive,' he said. 'Very impressive, I should imagine. And where are you off to, Justine, all dressed up without an escort?'

'Off to meet my secret lover, of course. You wouldn't expect me to have him pick me up at work.' The words simply hurtled from her mouth without conscious thought, and she shut her mouth immediately, more startled than even he could have been. Whatever could have possessed her to say such a thing?

Wyatt's eyes narrowed dangerously, or was it just a trick of the questionable light? Justine wasn't altogether sure, but there was little doubt about the harshness in his voice.

'Secret lover? Or just one who doesn't care enough about you to pick you up at home?' There wasn't much emphasis on his use of *home* as opposed to her *work*, but enough!

'What are you—my father or something?' Justine replied tartly. 'Surely you don't think it's part of your position as my employer to go about vetting my boy-friends?'

'That isn't very likely when you insist on running off to meet them in secret like . . .' He broke it off there, but the implication was obvious. Justine's temper flared.

'Like what?' she demanded. 'Like some kind of tart, perhaps? Or did you have a better, more descriptive word?'

'Maybe I didn't have any word at all,' he returned blithely. 'Perhaps I was merely going to say, *like this*?'

'And perhaps I'm the Queen of England,' she snapped. 'Now if you'll excuse me . . .'

'But of course,' he replied with an exaggerated but none the less graceful bow. 'I'm sure your . . . secret lover will appreciate your devotedness. Do I take it you'll be back for tomorrow's apprentices' dinner?'

'I don't know yet,' Justine replied angrily. 'Not that it's any of your business anyway. Besides, Armand will be here.'

'And so, I'd suggest, will you,' Wyatt replied. And his voice was grimly prophetic.

'I will if it damned well suits me, and not otherwise!' she cried, then jammed her foot on the accelerator and nearly ran over his foot in her haste to get away.

Hateful, arrogant man! How dared he suggest such things, she thought? Well, it would serve him right if she *did* stay out all night. Maybe she would! She could certainly find a hotel room; on Wyatt's wages she could even afford to, but it would be a horrifically expensive gesture.

By the time she had reached the restaurant, Justine's temper had cooled and she was able to greet Peter, who had arrived only moments before her, with a welcoming, genuine smile.

'You look ravishing,' he said, and his eyes revealed it to be no lie. 'I may have to change my mind and not go back to Melbourne at all.'

'Oh, but what would Sue say?' Justine laughed. She felt much better, although Wyatt's inquisition still rankled beneath the surface, and she was certain this would be an enjoyable, no-hassle evening, despite Peter's attentiveness.

And it was! Upon being introduced to Sebastian, Peter insisted that they place themselves entirely in the Greek's hands where the food was concerned, although he drew the line at nothing to drink but ouzo and insisted on a good wine.

Both of them thoroughly enjoyed Possum's first performance of the evening, which was a series of Greek and English folk songs that started off very gently and grew to rafter-shattering, riotous audience involvement towards the end.

Then it was time for dancing, and Justine was more than ready for a bit of exercise after four courses of Sebastian's chosen delicacies.

'I don't know how we're going to cope,' she told Peter. 'He says there are four more courses to come, and I haven't even got room for a cup of coffee.'

He laughed. 'We'll just have to dance it off, I guess. Although I must say I agree with you. The tucker's magnificent, but Sebastian must reckon we're laying in for a siege or something.'

Peter was, as Justine had quite expected, an excellent dancer. The music was fast and enjoyable, and within moments of being on the dance floor both she and her escort were fully into the spirit of things. They danced through several long sets before deciding it was time for a break, then returned to their table to find it was transformed from a table for two to one at which another couple were already in residence.

Justine felt her heart sink as they looked up. Gloria Calder shot her a defiantly possessive smirk, but Wyatt merely smiled pleasantly as he rose to welcome them.

'I was sure you wouldn't mind us joining you,' he said with a bow to Justine. 'It seems like one of those times when great minds think alike.'

Peter was genuinely glad to see Wyatt, but Justine had no illusions. She had seen through his welcoming smile, a smile that had done nothing to hide the black anger in his already dark eyes. Wyatt was furious! What she didn't know, but expected to find out all too soon, was why.

CHAPTER SEVEN

'JUST what the hell are you playing at, anyway?'

Wyatt's voice grated in Justine's ear. He'd wasted no time in finding the opportunity to speak to her; she had had time for only a sip of her drink and a cigarette before he had suggested—in tones that brooked no argument—that they dance.

Now he was holding her in a grip of steel, his fingers tight around hers and his arm around her waist holding her much too closely for comfort.

'I don't know what you mean,' she replied softly. 'And I do wish you'd stop trying to crush in my ribs.'

'You know damned well what I mean,' he snarled, and his arm, if anything, closed more tightly around her. 'Or hasn't dear Peter bothered to tell you he's spoken for?'

'What does that have to do with anything? Not that it's any of your business in the first place,' she whispered, having to struggle to get the words out and breathe at the same time.

'Don't you listen?' he muttered. 'I'm telling you that Peter is virtually engaged . . . to be married . . . to a girl in Melbourne.'

'I heard you the first time,' Justine grunted. 'But it has nothing to do with me.'

'I wouldn't have thought you the type to play about with somebody else's man,' he said, his voice still harsh in her ear.

'And I wouldn't have thought you the type to be running around interfering in things that are none of your business,' she retorted, struggling vainly against the pressure of his arm. She could feel the strength of

his body against her, the heat of his anger flowing between them like a boiling river.

Damn the man anyway, Justine thought. She could
end this by simply admitting she knew very well about
Peter's engagement and informing Wyatt that they
were only friends in any event. But I won't, she
thought. Let him think what he pleases.

'Anyone who works for me is my business,' he
growled in reply, 'especially when they start messing
about with my friends.'

'I am not messing about, as you so crudely put it,'
she snapped.

'And what else do you call sneaking off to meet
somebody you've barely met?'

'Sneaking? Are you right out of your tiny little
mind?' Justine demanded, now growing honestly
angry. How could he possibly accuse her so blatantly?
She managed then to shove herself far enough away
that she could peer up at him, unable to believe what
she had heard. 'Since when is it being sneaky to meet
somebody in a public restaurant?' she demanded.

'It's pretty obvious, I'd say,' he replied. 'Or have
you got some logical reason for your secret lover not
picking you up at home, openly and above board?'

'Oh, my God,' Justine cried. 'Don't tell me you took
that remark seriously?'

'Not until I walked in here and saw the evidence
with my own eyes,' he said. 'Not that it matters to
you, obviously.'

'Obviously,' Justine agreed. She was suddenly very
sick of arguing with this man, and already part of her
mind was concerned with her awareness of his physical
presence, the hardness of his body against hers, the
warmth of him. Instead of fighting his grip, she relaxed
into it, letting herself flow against him to the music.

If only, she thought, Wyatt would have the good
sense to just drop the argument, to simply dance with
her, hold her—but after a moment of silence she once

again heard that hateful growl in her ear.

'I suppose you were planning to spend the night with him as well?'

'Oh! Oh, shut up!' she snapped, this time so loudly that it drew them several interested stares from those dancing closest to them.

'That's not much of an answer,' he commented, blithely ignoring everyone but Justine.

'Well, it's all the answer you're likely to get,' she said. 'How dare you go about asking questions like that?'

'I can dare any damned thing I want to; you should know that,' he replied.

'Well, just go right ahead and do it then,' she retorted.

'Maybe I should just ask Peter.' And there was steel in his voice. He'd do it; Justine knew he would.

'Be . . . my . . . guest!' she replied, drawing out the three words into a contemptuous statement.

'Hah!' There was a strange glint of satisfaction in his voice. 'You don't think I would, do you?'

'Frankly I couldn't care less,' Justine muttered in reply.

'You could, you know. It would be . . . slightly embarrassing for you, to say the least.'

'Not in the slightest,' she replied. 'Shall we go and find out? I'm getting quite fed up with being mauled out here on the dance floor.'

'Nobody's mauling you,' he said. 'I just like to dance close, that's all.'

'Well, may I suggest you try it with Gloria? I'm sure she would appreciate the effort.'

'And you don't?' Wyatt's fingers suddenly ran up the length of her spine in a flickering, sensual motion that sent shivers through Justine's body. Then he dipped his head to run his lips across the softness of her neck.

'No,' she lied, 'I don't.' But her body betrayed her,

as Wyatt had very well known it would. Her nipples were erect against the warmth of his chest and her legs were like rubber, barely able to hold her upright against him.

'Please take me back to the table now,' she pleaded.

He chuckled mischievously. 'And if I don't? What are you going to do—throw a tantrum?'

'I might very well kick you where it'll do the most good,' Justine threatened. It was an idle threat, but how could he know that?

'Try it and I'll take you over my knee and paddle your pretty little rump for you,' he whispered in a voice that said *his* was no such idle threat.

The music ended there, but Wyatt made no move to return to the table. He looked in that direction, but upon seeing that Peter had taken Gloria on to the dance floor, he simply ignored Justine's demand.

'Perhaps after this one,' he said as the soft strains of a slow, sensuous waltz began, and before she could reply Justine was swept back into his arms and away across the floor.

No words now; Wyatt was simply dancing, using his body to create in her the most kaleidoscopic emotions. She couldn't help but be carried along by the music, the smoothness of his skilled performance and the sheer rapture of his embrace. His right hand played a tune of its own along the softness at the base of her spine, his legs moved sensuously against hers in the turns, his lips played with the lobe of her ear and his breath was a gentle breeze in her hair.

It was heaven and hell combined. Justine knew he was deliberately toying with her but every nerve in her body cried out for him never to stop, to simply let the music go on for ever so that she could stay in his arms.

Never in her life had she danced with anyone to whom her body was so perfectly tuned, with whom she seemed to just exactly fit. It was as if she were dancing on air, without any contact with the floor or those who swirled anonymously about them.

Her hand strayed upward from his shoulder so that her fingers could twine in the hair at the back of his neck. Her nostrils were filled with the heathery, out-doors scent of his aftershave, and wherever their bodies touched she was instantly aware of the texture of him.

But all too soon it was over, and this time he held forth no arguments, but wordlessly guided her from the dance floor to arrive at the table in unison with Peter and Gloria.

Justine could feel the other woman's eyes on her, like those of a snake about to strike. Only snakes don't smile, and Gloria was definitely smiling, a lean, feline grin that was so close to being a snarl Justine almost flinched away from it.

They were hardly seated before Sebastian arrived ahead of a waitress so loaded with food trays that Justine thought she might sink beneath the burden. To her great surprise, Justine found she was ravenous, while Wyatt certainly didn't let his harsh words affect his appetite.

All four of them tucked into the servings with mini-mal conversation, only Justine aware of the undercur-rents that flashed back and forth between herself and Wyatt.

She just *knew* he was going to say something to Peter that would be, at least, embarrassing. And then, suddenly, she knew equally well he wouldn't! Wyatt would never demean himself in such a way—he was merely toying with her and had very nearly succeeded.

Nonetheless, she felt a great surge of relief when the meal finally ended and Peter declared his need to make an end of the evening in the interests of tomorrow's workload. Even more of a relief was that he waited until Wyatt and Gloria were on the dance floor, which allowed Justine to offer him a lift back to his hotel without enduring Wyatt's hard-eyed attention as she did so.

'Why not stay and enjoy yourself?' he urged in reply, and Justine nearly laughed at the ridiculousness of the suggestion. Enjoy herself? With Wyatt deliberately baiting her at every turn and Gloria looking daggers? Not likely!

And even less likely when she discovered a moment later that Wyatt had arbitrarily assumed responsibility for the bill, effectively making them his guests for the evening. Peter took that in his stride, waving an elaborate gesture of thanks to the still-dancing couple as he and Justine made their way towards the entrance.

It was no satisfaction to have Gloria wave a casual goodbye while Wyatt merely nodded sagely, never taking his dark eyes from Justine.

He might as well have shouted across the room at them. His eyes ordered her to remember that earlier dance floor conversation, defying her to disobey him, challenging her to forget if she could the touch of his hands and the arrogance of his commands.

Justine dropped Peter at his hotel and politely refused his half-hearted offer of a nightcap. He didn't object, having clearly expected her to refuse.

'What are the chances of being invited to your apprentices' dinner tomorrow night?' he asked quite unexpectedly. 'It's an idea I'd like to see implemented in our own chain, but Wyatt said I couldn't look in unless you gave your permission.'

'He didn't!' Justine couldn't help herself; the words just popped out in her total amazement at Wyatt saying such a thing.

'My very word he did. And he was firm about it, too,' was the reply. 'I don't know what's going on between you two, but I'd caution you not to confuse personal feelings with Wyatt's professional feelings about you. After you left us at dinner the other night he had nothing but praise for you, and he wasn't kidding.'

He paused, then continued with a wry grin, 'Mind you, he didn't look real pleased with you tonight. Or maybe it was me he was shirty with; I couldn't be quite sure.'

'A little of both,' said Justine with a chuckle, then laughed lightly as she went on, 'He thinks we're having an affair, you see, and since you're sort of engaged and he knows it, he's apparently decided that we've offended his sensibilities.'

Peter's laugh was infectious, but he sobered after a moment to caution Justine yet again. 'All this does is prove my theory,' he said. 'There *is* something between you, whether you want to admit it or not. So be warned—Wyatt is nobody you want to play games with; he plays rough and he plays to win. You'd only get hurt, and I wouldn't want to see that.'

'All there is between us is what's commonly called a personality clash,' Justine said. 'So don't start playing at being a matchmaker; I've got troubles enough.'

'I wouldn't dream of such a thing,' Peter replied with a smirk that shouted out the fact that he was lying in his teeth. Then he leaned over to kiss Justine lightly on the cheek and an instant later was out of the car and leaning inside for a final word. 'You drive carefully on the way home and I'll see you tomorrow afternoon,' he said, and was gone before she could caution him again about his obvious intentions.

It made her more than usually thoughtful as she began the long drive home. Peter was obviously going to continue some little private game of his own, just to stir his old friend up a little. But me, I'll be the meat in the sandwich, Justine thought. It wasn't a pleasant thing to look forward to.

She could lie to Peter about her feelings about Wyatt Burns. She could certainly lie to Wyatt—and would have to! But she knew it was the sheerest folly to start lying to herself.

And Justine knew only too well that her feelings for Wyatt were no passing fancy, no youthful puppy-love. Never had she met anyone who could so easily take over her emotions, creating depths of feeling she didn't really want to know about.

Wyatt could hurt her. Worse, he very likely would. And short of running away, giving up the job she loved, there was little she could do about it. Indeed, she realised that she couldn't run away, not if it meant leaving Wyatt's and its dark-eyed owner.

But dared she stay? The risk of being hurt was frightening and only too real.

She was well into the southern suburbs and no closer to any solutions to her inner conflicts, when her car suddenly gave a lurch, a hiccough, and died. No warning, no ominous rattles or strange noises from the wilderness beneath the hood—it simply died!

Justine managed to get herself together quickly enough to stamp on the clutch and steer the vehicle off the main travel lanes. She even remembered to turn off the lights and radio in case it was something as simple as her battery giving up. But when she had coasted to a relatively safe stop she found any attempt to re-start the car was futile.

'Oh . . . damn!' she cried aloud. After the emotionalism of her evening's sparring with Wyatt, this was just the final straw. To be stranded on a main road, in evening wear and with midnight only minutes away, could only be classed as a legitimate disaster.

It took all her will power to sit back, light a cigarette and force herself to try and relax while plotting some solution to the problem. She was a member of the automobile club, but what good could that do without a telephone from which to call for help? She had plenty of money, but no real idea of where might be the closest open service station, or phone booth, or anything useful.

Hitch-hike? No, she decided . . . or at least only as the last possible resort. But to walk anywhere on this stretch of highway would be equally foolish.

Her knowledge of motor mechanics was only just

sufficient to tell her that even opening the hood would be a waste of time without expert advice thereafter, but somehow it seemed an appropriate gesture, so she did it.

'Now what?' she asked herself, trying to ignore the more sinister aspects of the situation. All that would be needed to make things even worse would be a confrontation with a carload of passing louts; Justine tried to force *that* thought from her mind as she surveyed the passing traffic and wondered if she dared try to flag down some help.

Suddenly the night seemed darker, each approaching set of headlights like the eyes of some predatory animal. She fled back to sit in the small car, physically hiding despite a certain knowledge that she couldn't possibly just sit there until daylight.

A couple of times, motorists slowed to inspect her wounded vehicle, but nobody stopped of their own accord and Justine couldn't quite build up the nerve to step out and flag anyone down. She had almost reached that point, however, when the decision was made for her.

This car did stop, cruising in to park directly ahead of her. And fright quickly gave way to shivering relief when she saw the blue light on the roof and the uniformed patrolman who stepped out to approach her.

He was brusque but helpful, and, most important, he stayed with her until the motoring club service vehicle arrived. There, things steadily went from bad to worse.

She didn't fully understand what the mechanic was telling her, except that it was something serious enough that he couldn't fix it on the spot. It would have to be towed to the workship he said, and she might be lucky enough to have it back by noon the next day.

He couldn't, unfortunately, leave his own district to give her a ride all the way south to Wyatt's, but at least he could offer a lift to where she could get a taxi or arrange accommodation.

Justine rode with him back to his service depot, suddenly conscious of her flimsy dress and the man's appreciative glances. Once there, she dealt with the required paperwork and waited what seemed like forever for a taxi.

The taxi driver quoted her a price that made her reel with shock; she had forgotten just how far south of the city proper Wyatt's really was. She was tempted to tell him she only wanted to rent his car, not buy it, but she thought better of that instinct and decided instead to just cut her losses and book into the most convenient hotel.

It wasn't until she was safely ensconced in a tidy, comfortable and expensive hotel room that the reaction began to set in and her earlier fears and trials gave way to relieved laughter at the immense chain of misfortune.

She remembered thinking of booking into a hotel during her drive into the city, and had to laugh at the prophecy in those thoughts.

Pouring herself a drink from the hotel room's well-stocked mini-fridge, she sat down on the edge of the bed and reviewed the night's events with growing amusement. Would Wyatt be waiting, she wondered, making all sorts of ridiculous assumptions about her failure to arrive?

She got a mental flash of him, sitting on the steps of his own restaurant in the middle of the night like the parent of some errant teenager. And again she laughed.

'It would just about serve you right,' she muttered aloud.

And it would, too. How dared he try and run her life? It was none of his business what she did, or with whom, or when she came in after a date. None of his business, yet she was curiously flattered despite her innate hostility at being ordered about.

Why should he care anyway? Clearly he had no great interest in her from any romantic viewpoint, despite Peter's claims to the contrary. Physical interest? That she couldn't deny; the memories of his caresses were just too strong.

But that, Justine decided, simply wasn't enough. She didn't need or want to be used by Wyatt or any other man as a convenience, a sex object. And how close she'd been, on that memorable occasion in her flat, to becoming just that!

She glanced at her watch. Almost one in the morning. If Wyatt actually was keeping tabs on her, he'd be going without sleep. Just as she was, but that was little consolation for being too keyed up to sleep.

'I wonder if perhaps I should telephone,' she mused—and then dismissed the thought. It was none of his business where she spent the night, and Justine was damned if she'd give him the satisfaction of seeing his heavy-handed threats actually working.

But if she didn't telephone, he might think she'd stayed over with Peter. Did she have the right to let her own feelings cause bad relations between friends? Not that Peter would mind, she thought; he obviously quite enjoyed stirring Wyatt up.

And yet . . . Before she had time to change her mind, Justine grabbed up her handbag, looked up the private number of the telephone in Wyatt's flat, and quickly dialled it.

One ring . . . two . . . and the phone was answered. Only not by Wyatt! Justine nearly dropped the telephone when Gloria's unmistakable voice came through.

'I'd like to speak to Wyatt, please,' said Justine, half wishing she'd simply hung up without a word.

'I'm sorry, but you can't. He's . . . occupied right now,' was the reply. Gloria had recognised Justine's voice, too, no question about that.

'I . . . see,' she replied. 'Well, could you please tell

him that I've had car trouble and I might not be back until tomorrow afternoon?' The words came hard for her, and Justine suddenly felt herself like the errant teenager of her earlier vision. How ridiculous it all seemed!

Gloria's reply was mumbled. Justine couldn't quite decide if it was a yes, no, maybe, or just what. And before she could ask, the phone was hung up in her ear.

She sat there, dumbstruck by the outright rudeness and still holding the now-buzzing receiver, which she looked at as if it were something unusual.

'Well!' she exlaimed as she replaced the receiver. And then again . . . 'Well!' It wasn't until some time later, when she had undressed and sprawled beneath the coverlet on the wide double bed, that the frustration and anger came pouring in.

Clearly she didn't have to worry about Wyatt Burns. He was quite obviously taking care of his needs without any help from her. And with Gloria! Well, it was hardly unexpected. The other woman's hostility towards Justine had to be based on something.

The hypocrite! She shuddered at the nerve of a man who would so arrogantly dictate *her* behaviour while putting a quite different standard on his own. And why? Did he get some big emotional thrill from toying with her emotions? Surely he couldn't be that brutally callous.

And yet, she realised, he might very well be. It was only her own feelings about Wyatt that made her question it, because in her heart she didn't want to believe him that callous.

It hadn't been her concern for Peter that had prompted the phone call. It had been her own desire for Wyatt to think well of her, to care! Because she loved him, and she could no longer deny the fact at all—not even under the harsh, painful reality that it was a love which meant nothing at all to him.

But how could she possibly love someone who cared so little? It seemed ludicrous, but it was undeniable, and when sleep took her, finally, Justine still had no proper answer.

The next morning dawned bright and sunny and warm, the perfect day for a sail on Sydney Harbour, or a walk in the park or anything but work. It was also the complete opposite of how Justine felt inside. She had slept long, but poorly, and woke with a raging headache and a bitter emptiness inside her.

The only bright spot was that her car repairs weren't terribly expensive, although it was after noon when the repairs were finally completed and she had been forced to wait nearly two hours at the service depot, sitting on an uncomfortable chair and feeling quite ridiculous in evening wear.

As she turned back on to the highway and headed south, every instinct cried out to her to turn round, go away, anywhere . . . anywhere but back to Wyatt's where she could find only heartache.

But she had to go, and by the time she arrived Justine had reconciled herself both to facing Wyatt Burns and to the questionable pleasure of yet another apprentices' dinner. The Monday night sessions had seemed an excellent idea when she had started, but the novelty was beginning to pall. And on this, of all days, she felt she would need every bit of intestinal fortitude she could muster.

Wyatt was standing on the front porch when she turned in at the drive. Could it be otherwise? she thought. 'This will just make my day,' she muttered, debating whether to slip in through the back or brave the lion at the front entry.

As she garaged the car, Justine kept looking over her shoulder, half expecting Wyatt to storm into the garage and resume his harangue. But he didn't, and although the rear entrance to the building was overwhelmingly tempting, she steeled herself and strode round to the front, shoulders back and head held high in a mixture of defiance and pride.

She had to force herself to meet his eyes, eyes that were like wet black stones, expressionless and cold and somehow menacing.

'Good afternoon.' The words were friendly enough, but he spat them out as if they tasted bad, and there was no smile, no hint of true welcome.

Justine replied calmly, wondered if she ought to say anything else, then decided against it. Wyatt certainly didn't care; he was holding open the door for her, but his manner was that of someone who didn't want to be soiled.

Well, the same to you! she thought, sweeping through the open doorway with every ounce of dignity she possessed. There was a horrible, childish temptation to turn and confront him, to jeer and chant, 'I know what you're thinking, but you're wrong. So there! And I don't care anyway.'

The words swarmed into her mind so loudly that for an instant she feared she actually *had* shouted them, but when she turned at the foot of the stairway it was to face only the door, now closed between them.

But the words remained, turning over and over in a repetitious litany as she climbed the staircase. I don't care anyway . . . I don't care . . . I don't care . . . I don't care . . .

Which would have been just fine, except that she *did* care, and couldn't change that for anything. Instead of going straight in to change, Justine leaned at the top of the staircase, her legs suddenly heavy as lead, heavy as her heart. She stayed for a moment, looking out, gathering fresh reserves of strength, and was about to continue when the taxi arrived and she saw Peter step out, obviously waving a greeting to Wyatt.

'If I'd known you were coming this early I could have given you a lift myself,' she said to no one in particular, then strode away to her flat and the pleasant chore of getting changed.

She unlocked the heavy door, stepped inside, and had only just closed the door behind her when it suddenly flung open to crash against the wall.

Into the room marched the figure of her employer, and if Wyatt's eyes had been cold down on the front porch, they were the extreme opposite now. He slammed the door shut and strode over to take Justine by the shoulders, his fingers biting through the softness of her flesh.

'You little bitch!' he snarled, so fiercely that she would have flinched in fear of a blow, had she been able to move at all.

One hand released her, raised in the air like a club, but he somehow gained a measure of control, for it stopped, trembling in his anger, without actually striking her.

Justine could only stand there, shocked and horrified beyond speech. Even her mind wouldn't work.

Wyatt's eyes blazed in fury and she could see the muscles of his throat and jaw throbbing. When he finally spoke again, however, his voice was deathly soft, fearsome in its softness. 'And I suppose you haven't got a thing to say,' he asked in a question that wasn't. 'My God, but you're a cold bitch!'

Cold? Goodness, but she was cold! It seemed as if she'd been deep frozen. Especially her tongue, which seemed to fill her mouth but couldn't make an intelligible sound.

Wyatt looked at her, disgust alive in his eyes. 'I suppose you did it purely to spite me,' he hissed. 'Or was it just for the thrill of taking somebody else's man?'

'What?' It was the only word she could utter, and even it struggled lamely around her dry and lifeless tongue.

'What? Damn it, woman, do you take me for a fool? Why in the hell didn't you just drive Peter back here yourself, instead of this little charade with the taxi? I'm surprised he could afford it, after paying you for your night's . . . work.'

Justine gasped. The reality of his charges struck her like an axe, but no more quickly than her free hand lashed out to bruise itself against his granite jaw.

It hurt! Not like the pain inside her, but it hurt enough to free her tongue. 'Get out!' she snapped, and her trembling now was anger, not fear any more. 'You . . . you bastard—*get out!*'

As well shriek at the moon. Wyatt stood immobile, his eyes blazing down at her like those of a raging beast, his broad chest heaving as he fought for control. Never in her life had Justine ever seen anyone so angry.

'Well,' he said finally, 'at least you aren't lying and trying to deny it. I suppose that's something.'

'Why should I bother? You wouldn't believe me anyway.'

'Too right I wouldn't! What I can't understand is why. *Why?* You knew Peter was taken; I told you myself. Surely to God you're not *that* hard up . . . '

'That hard up? And just how hard up does one have to be to appreciate the attentions of a decent, proper gentleman—something you never have been and never damned well will be?'

Justine was in full temper herself now. She wouldn't have denied the charge for anything. Let him think what he wanted.

'I think you've got a nerve,' she cried. 'You're nothing but a chauvinist, double-standard . . . bastard! It's fine for you to spend the night with whatever female is dumb enough to accommodate you, but you're all fired up about what I do—which happens, I remind you, to be none of your business in the first place.'

He might have replied then, but she didn't give him a chance. 'What's the real reason for the complaint?' she demanded, all reason gone now. 'Jealous because somebody else got what you didn't—and damned well never will get?'

Wyatt's face darkened in a flush of fresh anger, and for a second Justine thought he really *would* hit her. His fingers tightened on her shoulder until she thought the bone would snap.

'I don't have to content myself with another man's leavings,' he sneered, and the teeth that flashed were those of a wolf. Justine's throat tightened instinctively at the sight of them, but her blood was fairly up and she no longer knew or cared what she was saying.

'Hmph! You probably couldn't handle it anyway,' she sneered in return, her own look as scornful as his was angry. Let him strike her. In fact she rather wanted him to; it would perhaps distil her inner feelings for him, make her less vulnerable.

But he didn't hit her. And when he finally spoke it was in a whisper so threatening that the words bored into her brain. 'By God, but you're a maddening bitch,' he grated, 'but now you've gone too far!'

And before Justine could think to stop him, he had dragged her into his arms, his mouth descending upon hers with a savagery which she couldn't hope to oppose.

He was so quick, so strong, and so merciless. His arms pinned her own to her sides, his strong hands pulled her against him so firmly she could barely breathe and he easily countered her attempts to fight back.

When she tried to kick, he thrust his leg between hers and crushed her against him until she gasped for breath; her arms stayed pinioned as he ravaged her mouth.

Justine's mouth softened under his assault, opening like a flower as his breath mingled with hers, as the taste of him penetrated her palate, the heady scent of him seared into her flaring nostrils. Her lips were bruised, but that could not stop her from reacting to his kisses.

And he knew! Instinctively, it seemed, he knew exactly when he could safely release her arms, giving his own hands freedom to explore her body, stroking upon tender nerves and flaring her own desires to unquenchable heights.

Her breasts hardened with arousal as his fingers touched them through the fine fabric of her gown, her tummy trembled at his touch and when his fingers moved lower, searching for and finding the core of her desire, she thought she would burst into flame.

When his lips released her mouth and began a pagan search along her throat, her own lips embarked on a search of their own across the roughness of his cheek, tasting the lobe of his ear, nuzzling into the hair on his neck. Her hands followed, holding him close to her, no longer fighting him, betraying her completely by roaming across his shoulders and into the rough texture of his hair as she held him.

He straightened slightly, forcing her arms to lift higher, and as she lifted with him, Justine felt the slither of her gown as he casually whipped it upward. There was only that split second when they didn't touch; she was in his arms again before the gown had landed where he'd thrown it. Only now she was naked but for her hose, and his relentless searching hands were like torches on her skin, striking fires of need and desire wherever they touched. Freed of restraint, his lips moved across her shoulders, down to where her turgid nipples strained for his kisses.

When he lifted his head to bring his mouth once again to hers, Justine's hands moved lower to pluck at the buttons of his shirt, baring his chest so that her fingers could nestle in the short crisp hair. She was moaning unintelligibly, aware now only of her desire, her reaction to Wyatt's caresses, her desperate, searing need of him.

He pulled her close, his hands like iron bands around her, and she could feel the heat, the hardness of his masculinity against her like a magnet of desire.

And then she was in his arms as he lifted her, carrying her to the enormous bed with his mouth trapping her own, his fingers caressing her even as he moved the few steps necessary.

The hose slipped away, it seemed, in the instant he laid her down and his lips, his hands, were everywhere, lifting her to peaks of desire she had never believed possible.

And her own hands were as busy, stripping the shirt from him, roaming down across his chest and stomach, thrilling in the touch of muscles, down . . . down across the fabric of his trousers.

All thought of resistance was long vanished; Justine wanted only fulfilment, wanted only the satiation of her desires. She wanted him!

Her mind was numbed, her lips swollen with his kisses. Only her senses were alive, and as his caress became increasingly intimate, Justine rose higher and higher on a sweeping plane of desire.

It was heaven and hell rolled into one. She wanted his caresses never to cease, but she wanted even more the totality of their union, the joining of their bodies despite the barrier between their hearts and minds.

And as her desires escalated, she wanted only him, without question, without conditions, without commitment. He would take her and she would not only comply, but she would—she was already doing it—help him, encourage him, love him.

But Wyatt would not love her. He would only take her, gaining his revenge upon her in the most satisfactory and most devastating of manners. Justine didn't care any more. Whether it was revenge or anger or simple animal need, she wanted him, needed him.

And he wanted her, no longer any question of that. His caresses had ceased to be harsh, brutal. Now they were skilled and delicate and tender . . . almost loving.

And finished! Even as she relaxed herself for that final, total submission, he was gone. No word, no warning, and certainly no apology. The instant she reached the pinnacle, the ultimate, absolute summit of her need, Wyatt simply let her go, got up and walked away.

Discarded shirt dangling from his hand, he was across the room and out the door, even closing it softly behind him, before the first tear fell.

CHAPTER EIGHT

IT was a lifetime before Justine could move, an eternity before the well of tears ran dry and her discarded body once again began to regain a semblance of life.

She managed, somehow, to get herself into the bathroom and under the stinging needles of the shower without having to face herself in any mirror, and she stood there like a drooping flower as the water vainly tried to wash away the soil of Wyatt's scorn.

She soaped and rinsed and soaped again, laving every inch of her skin, double-shampooing her hair, but still the touch of him was on her. It would be, she realised, for ever.

And she hated him. Hated him with all the passion that had earlier throbbed with love and caring and need. She wanted to kill him, destroy, chop him into minuscule pieces. She wanted to see him suffer, to see her own revenge as strong and as hateful and as hurtful as his had been.

But she didn't want ever to see him again. And as she listlessly sat drying her hair, spending nearly an hour at the thankless task, she knew she had no real alternative.

Already she was late for the cooking activities in the kitchens below. She couldn't, much as she wanted it, simply walk away from Wyatt's with the tattered shreds of her pride. She had a responsibility to her students, to her customers, and even, she supposed, to herself.

So she wasn't yet through with Wyatt's, although she would certainly do her best to ensure that she was through with Wyatt himself. Somewhere inside her an icy veneer was already forming over her shame, cloak-

ing her humiliation in a freezing covering that would
protect her.

When she finally dressed and hurried down the long
staircase, only her eyes and the bruised softness of
her mouth were visual evidence of how she felt inside.

And, luckily, she reached the kitchen without Wyatt
in it, and even without meeting him on the way. She
was greeted enthusiastically by her staff, though she
noticed that most of them turned away quickly, returning to their work and even making unnecessary
work because it meant they didn't have to say anything
about her obvious wounding.

Only Peter could do that, and he was wise enough to
say nothing. But his eyes showed that he, too, had
noticed, and that he was concerned and worried, but
too sensitive to intrude on what was so obviously private.

Instead, he did his best to buoy up her spirits with
news, good news from his viewpoint and therefore
good news for Justine, although Wyatt might have dis-
agreed.

'Damned good thing you got me home when you
did, last night.' he chuckled. 'You'll never guess what
I found waiting for me when I got to my room.'

Justine, too emotional to think clearly, made the
required three guesses without much spirit, but
laughed delightedly when he announced the real
answer.

'Sue!' And his happiness glowed like an inner lamp.
'She got in not five minutes ahead of me. I was going
to bring her along today. She wants to meet you, of
course, but I wasn't sure of the house rules about extra
visitors. Besides, she had relatives to visit today, so
we're coming out to dinner one night this week. And
on Sunday, when you can be free, I'd like to take both
of you—and Wyatt, of course—out to dinner somewhere different.'

'Oh, Peter . . . I . . . I just can't promise that,' she replied, knowing he wouldn't understand because she couldn't tell him. 'But certainly come here one night. I'd love to meet Sue, I really would. If only to tell her how extremely lucky I think she is.'

'Flattery will get you anywhere,' he grinned. 'And now I'll leave you for a bit. I've got a touch of business to talk over with Wyatt, but I'll see you when the meal's ready.'

'All right,' she said. And then, as he was halfway to the door, 'Peter! Hang on a minute. I've . . . a favour to ask. It's very presumptuous, but I . . . I just must.'

'You want to know if that job offer's still open? Of course it is, more than ever. Except I presume you'll want to be joining our Melbourne operation, not stay in Sydney?'

Justine smiled. How very understanding, how kind he was. 'I do think Melbourne would be better,' she replied softly.

'Your privilege,' he said with a shake of his head. 'Do you want me to broach the subject with Wyatt? I will, despite it being against my better judgment.'

'N . . . no, I think that's something I'll have to do myself,' Justine faltered. 'If I can, that is, and I guess I'll have to.'

'It would probably be best,' he agreed, 'but if I get a chance I'll mention to him that I'm going to make every attempt to steal you away. Don't worry, I won't even mention we've talked about it, but it might make your task a bit easier when the time comes if he knows there's seriousness on both sides.'

Obviously he didn't get such an opportunity that afternoon or at least he said nothing during the apprentices' dinner that evening. The dinner was delightful, as good as Justine herself might have prepared. Which didn't explain at all why it tasted like sawdust and old rags instead of spicy, rich *cannelloni con ricotta.*

The only saving grace was Wyatt's absence. Without that, Justine thought, she'd not only have been unable to taste the food, she'd have been physically sick as well. Gloria, too, was absent, but Justine hardly noticed that except in passing.

She saw Wyatt once on Tuesday, twice on Wednesday and again on Thursday, but on none of those occasions did he speak to her or even offer a greeting. His eyes were like ice chips and his manner hard, diamond-hard, as if his entire being was closed off against her.

Justine herself was an automaton. She did her work, tried her best to be pleasant when required, but in reality she was little more than a walking cooking machine, her life bounded by her kitchen and her upstairs flat.

It wasn't until the Friday evening, when Peter brought his Sue to dinner at Wyatt's, that Justine's own personal prison was forcibly shattered.

It was no surprise that they were coming; she had had a personal phone call from Peter to arrange both their booking and their preferences. These, he said, were 'entirely up to you—Chef's Choice.'

Justine spent most of the afternoon on a wide range of speciality dishes, was pleasantly satisfied when each one turned out exactly as she had planned, and was even more pleased when she got the message that Peter would like her to come and meet Sue whenever she could break free.

The only bad part was that Wyatt, as she might have expected but hadn't, was already with Peter and Sue at their table.

Justine halted in her tracks. They hadn't seen her yet, could she possibly make a retreat, send some flimsy excuse to put off the occasion? Too late. Wyatt, at least, had seen her, although his fathomless black eyes gave no hint of recognition.

That alone didn't matter, but she knew he would wreak a horrible vengeance if she had the rudeness and temerity to snub his friends—and hers—at this point.

Blow him! The thought echoed over and over in her mind as she squared her shoulders and advanced on the table. She had to forcibly restrain it, in fact, lest those be the first words to escape when she opened her mouth.

'Justine!' Peter rose to his feet and took her hand, bending to kiss it with his usual gallantry and then immediately introducing Justine to his Sue. Wyatt didn't even rise from his seat, and Justine, determined she could be as ruthlessly cold as he, blankly ignored his presence as if he didn't exist.

For Sue, however, she had a warm and friendly smile that was honestly and genuinely returned.

'I'm horribly jealous of you,' Sue said immediately, and from the corner of her eye Justine caught a self-satisfied smirk growing on Wyatt's lips.

'I am, you know.' the younger girl continued. 'Peter has talked so much about you that I shouldn't be jealous, especially after you were so kind on Sunday night and sent him off just in time to meet me. I wasn't jealous then, of course, but now that I've seen you I'm surprised he went home at all.'

Realisation of what she'd said made Sue blush vividly. 'Oh, that wasn't what I meant at all,' she gushed. 'It's just that . . . oh, I'm making a horrible muddle! I always do.'

'I wouldn't worry about it,' Justine replied with a smile as she forced herself not to look, even for an instant, towards Wyatt. 'Both of us had already had a long, long day on Sunday, so an early night was really called for. I'm just pleased it turned out so well for you two.'

There was the slightest emphasis there, not enough to alert or alarm Sue, or even Peter. But Wyatt caught it, Justine's peripheral vision picked up just the slightest flicker of taut neck muscle.

'Oh, it certainly did,' Sue replied with another, this time very revealing blush. 'I was so sorry to hear about your problems, though. It must have been terribly frightening, being stranded like that in the middle of the night.'

'And then to have to book into a hotel,' Peter added. 'Really, Justine, I'm still a bit angry that you didn't telephone me instead; we could have arranged something. At the very least you might have phoned Wyatt; he's usually quite good in emergencies.'

Justine grinned. Her inner resources were suddenly alive with sheer, lovely vengeance. Wyatt was almost visibly squirming in his seat now. He knew! He knew now that all of his accusations were false, that his . . . his rape of that afternoon, however unconsummated, was totally unjustified.

To hell with him! 'Wyatt,' she said without so much as a glance in Wyatt's direction, 'was quite obviously too busy that evening to be worrying about me. Besides, I'm pretty hard, according to some people. I could cope and I did.'

Squirm, you devil. Squirm and wriggle, and I hope you die, she thought. But don't you dare try to apologise, not now—not ever. Because I'll throw it in your face.

'Well, I have to admit I was surprised when I arrived on Monday and found you'd only just got here ahead of me,' Peter told her. 'You could have saved me the cab fare, not that I couldn't afford it or anything.'

Justine had a ready reply, and although she ached to throw it out like a slap in Wyatt's face, she didn't. She couldn't, not without possibly hurting Sue or Peter, and she wasn't prepared to debase her friendship just for a crack at Wyatt.

'Well, it all worked out satisfactorily in the end,' she

quipped finally—and was mightily amused to see that even *that* seemed to register with Wyatt.

Justine looked in his direction then, not at him, but past him to where Possum hovered expectantly. It took only a slightly raised eyebrow to have Possum scampering for fresh drinks for the table and a glass of Justine's favourite wine for the chef, and Justine returned her attention to Peter and Sue without even having to meet Wyatt's eyes.

Again, it was Sue with her youthful, innocent enthusiasm who picked up the conversation and once again afforded Justine a vengeful comment.

'I have to say that I just loved the interview you did with that . . . oh, what's her name? It doesn't matter anyway, because what I wanted to say was that I found your description of Wyatt a bit . . . much?'

'Oh, I thought it was quite tame, myself,' Justine replied. 'But then there's a limit to the kind of language you can use in a family publication.'

Sue's eyes widened. Then she smiled. 'Oh, you're just joking, of course,' she said. 'Even after all Peter's told me, I can't imagine Wyatt being *that* much of a chauvinist.'

'Oh, he hides it well . . . rather like his age,' Justine replied. And while everyone but herself laughed, Wyatt's laughter was hollow, chilling and dangerous.

'What Justine really means is that I'm somewhat intolerant,' he said, speaking up for the first time. 'She finds it very very easy to remember that I was, admittedly, opposed to hiring a female chef. But she just as easily *forgets* that I *did* hire her, regardless of my better judgment, and that I only occasionally regret it.'

Like now, I'll bet, Justine thought angrily. But she didn't have to speak, because Wyatt still held the floor.

'It's just unfortunate that she doesn't forgive as easily as she forgets,' he said, and she was somehow impelled to meet the fire of his eyes. And fire there was! His eyes were fairly blazing with an unholy, diabolical light.

Was he trying to tell her something? Well, too bad, she thought. I don't even want to know. But she did know. His words might have been generally directed at his audience, but they were aimed solely at her.

'Actually,' she said, speaking very, very carefully, 'Wyatt isn't nearly as bad as some bosses I've known. A friend of mine once got tangled up with a boss who had the nerve to accuse her of sleeping with one of his friends. Her boss had seen her out with the fellow, but he didn't realise that on her way home she'd had a car breakdown, much like mine. She was late for work next day and he went totally off his brain with accusations.'

She paused so long, not only for effect but to cautiously structure her thoughts, that Sue broke in to ask what had happened.

'She must have been *furious*,' said Sue, but Justine noticed Peter sliding back in his seat so that his lady's figure hid his own face from Wyatt. *He* knew. And so did Wyatt, of course. If looks could kill I'd be dead, thought Justine.

'Oh, it wasn't too bad,' she continued. 'She was a bit of a cold fish anyway. She merely stood up to him as best she could, then got even later. She fed him mushrooms—*poisoned* mushrooms.'

There was a gasp from Peter, who immediately grabbed up his napkin to cover his face. 'Sorry,' he said when he finally emerged all red in the face. 'Bit of wine went down the wrong way, that's all.' Wyatt seemed not to notice, but Justine, who could hardly keep a straight face herself, went in mortal terror for the next few moments, afraid Peter would break up entirely.

He nearly did, too, when his fiancée, either amazingly perceptive or startlingly naïve—Justine thought it likely the former—turned to Wyatt and asked with a perfectly straight face, 'Aren't you glad now that you don't like mushrooms, Wyatt?'

Give the devil his due, Justine thought as she struggled with every vestige of control to keep from giggling herself, Wyatt Burns was cool. Better than cool. He never so much as cracked a smile as he replied with equal calm.

'Actually, Sue, I had been starting to develop a taste for them,' he said. 'But I think Justine has rather put me off them again, at least for the moment.'

And he looked squarely at Justine, a look of haughty superiority that screamed 'Nyah!' in total silence. It was as if he was daring her to keep trying to needle him.

Too bad, mate. I don't do anything that you want, she thought, and immediately dropped all the word games and began making noises about returning to her duties.

'Don't be silly, Justine,' Wyatt snapped before anyone else could speak. 'All your main courses are done and if you're needed they know damned well where you are, anyway.'

It was an order, and a poorly disguised one at that, judging from Peter's flickering eyebrows. 'I told you so, even warned you,' said his expression, and Justine replied with a look that shouted quite clearly, 'And I wish I'd listened.'

But the look she gave Wyatt held no such message. Nor did her voice when she finally spoke. 'Well, if it's going to be a party, perhaps you'd allow me to slip up and change,' she said. 'Or would you rather I just stayed and felt silly dressed like this?'

Oh, that horrid, wolfish grin! Teeth . . . the better to eat you with, my dear. And that half-raised eyebrow, mocking, sceptical, alluring.

'Perhaps you'd like me to see you safely upstairs,' he said, and the innuendo dripped like venom . . . or was it nectar?

The look Justine shot him was one of pure, undiluted contempt. Wasn't it? Well, it was supposed to be, although his face didn't reveal much.

'Oh, I don't think there's any great danger,' she said, and added silently, 'so long as you're down here.' And he heard it, silent or no. There was a single flash of anger in those eyes.

At least, she thought, this time *both* Peter and Wyatt rose politely at her departure. She fled to her room and quickly unpinned her hair, shrugging it into a golden cloud as she reached into the wardrobe to pull out the dress. *The* dress, the same silky caftan Wyatt had so skilfully removed from her during his attack on Monday.

She was back in the dining room within minutes, striding through the room with an unexpected but exciting awareness that every man in the room was staring as she passed.

Even Wyatt! Especially Wyatt, and he wasn't only just staring; he was getting her message loud and clear and straight. And Justine wished she could shout it at him, right out loud, despite it being so obscene she felt uncomfortable even thinking in such language.

When he politely rose to hold out her chair, she stayed resolutely on her feet until he finally let go of it, allowing her to seat herself at only the cost of a black scowl as he slid into his own chair.

And the same to you, she thought, smiling at him in a gesture that deliberately added insult to injury.

The rest of the evening fairly flew past, with Peter, Sue and Justine doing virtually all of the talking while Wyatt grew increasingly withdrawn. Not that he visibly displayed his moodiness; he seemed merely content to sit back and let the others carry the conversation.

It meant that Justine was deprived of further opportunities to needle him, which she had already decided to do in any event, but it didn't stop Peter.

Justine stopped Peter. This was her game, she decided, and at his first attempt to slip in a sly dig at Wyatt she so positively deflected his attempt that he immediately got the message.

They sat until the restaurant was virtually empty, and it wasn't until Wyatt casually suggested that they could dance if anyone was interested that Justine felt the first flutterings of panic.

Dance? Not for the world would she allow herself to be placed in a position where she would be forced to let Wyatt so much as touch her.

'You carry on if it suits you,' she said with a negative shake of her head. 'I, on the other hand, am a working girl with another hard day tomorrow, so I'm afraid I'll have to call it a night.'

And Peter, bless his heart, picked up her lead and added his own regret that they, also, would have to end the evening. Only then he followed it with a suggestion for which Justine could cheerfully have wrung his neck.

'I don't want either of you to forget about Sunday night,' he said. 'I've found an ideal place for all of us to go to dinner, and I'll have no quibbles about it either. Fantastic food, from what I've heard, and a really good dance band. Agreed?'

The 'No!' that surged up in Justine's throat was drowned by Wyatt's quieter but verbal objection. 'I honestly can't promise, old mate,' he said before Justine could speak. 'I know Justine will be happy to join you, but I have a prior engagement that I simply can't break, so although I'll promise to do my best to join you before the evening's over, I honestly can't promise.'

Peter wasn't to be put off. 'Well, let's put it off until Monday, then,' he said. 'Surely you can get out of your junior cooking classes for one week?'

'She can, but I can't,' Wyatt pronounced, again before Justine had a chance. Then he turned to her with a slow smile that was almost apologetic. 'It's Possum's turn again, isn't it?' Justine nodded and he continued, turning back to Peter, 'There you have it. If I miss my darling sister's exhibition twice in a row, she'll never forgive me in a million years. No, let's leave it at Sunday and I'll do the best I can to arrive on time.'

Peter didn't look amused. 'And what about you, Justine? Have you got a great round of excuses too?'

She did—but Peter's hurt look instantly banished them. She really liked both him and Sue, and couldn't bear to hurt either of them.

On the other hand, she also had promised Possum faithfully to help with a magnificent production on Monday night, and she couldn't get out of that even knowing that Wyatt would be attending without fail.

'No,' she said. 'I've no excuses because you warned me about this earlier, remember? So Sunday night it is, and I warn you I'm expecting a meal that lives up to your advance billing.'

'Oh, that's asking a bit much,' he said, instantly grinning his pleasure at her acceptance. 'Even the best has to take second place to you in the cooking department, but I think this one'll just maybe manage that.'

And so it was arranged. Peter promised faithfully to phone the next day when he had confirmed the bookings, and Justine, fortunately, was allowed to bid her farewells there at the table and escape to her room while Wyatt was seeing Peter and Sue off.

She undressed, showered and got ready for bed, one ear cocked throughout for the half-expected knock on her door. Or would Wyatt have the nerve? After this evening she didn't really know what to expect, although she had enjoyed her small beginnings of revenge quite immensely.

She wasn't disturbed, however, and fell asleep wondering what she could arrange to further annoy him on Sunday night. There *must* be something. She felt strangely unfulfilled by her minor triumphs despite their momentary satisfactions.

On Saturday; she got a perfect opportunity. And from the most unexpected of sources—Wyatt himself!

Justine was tired after her late and emotionally exhausting night, and decided to slip upstairs for an hour's nap between the hurried lunchtime work and her start on the evening's preparations.

She unlocked the door to her suite, stifling a yawn as she stepped inside, already reaching for the zip on her white coverall. Then she stopped in her tracks, alerted by the scent of freshness, of new-cut flowers. She moved into the room cautiously, but she was quite alone.

Except, that was, for the largest bouquet of flowers she had ever seen. Her first reaction was a surge of real pleasure; it was a gesture typical of Peter, and she had no doubt he'd sent them in thanks for her extra efforts with the dinner for him and Sue the night before.

Then she saw the card. Then she saw red—literally! The red of roses, the flower of lovers, and the red ink in which Wyatt had written simply, 'I'm sorry.'

Damn the man! She'd seen him three times already that day, even spoken a polite good morning. If he wanted to apologise he could have done it then. But like this—without even a spoken word—the effort seemed forced and artificial.

Suddenly she recognised the slightly amused look she had noticed in his eyes earlier, the reason for the quick and ready smiles. Well, she'd give him something to smile about, exactly as he deserved!

It took Justine five minutes of sneaking round the building like a white-clad cat burglar before she could ascertain by some covert questioning that Wyatt was over at the market garden on some errand or another.

Perfect! It gave her sufficient time. Returning to her suite, she grabbed up the bouquet of flowers—had to use both hands to do it—and made her way sneakily down the staircase and hallway to his office.

It took more nerve than she had expected to actually reach out and open the door. She had to place the bouquet on the floor to give her a free hand, and every instinct shrieked the warning that when that door opened, Wyatt would be sitting behind his desk instead of away on his errand.

But he wasn't, and Justine quickly grabbed up the flowers, raced into the room and dumped the entire apology upside down in Wyatt's waste-paper basket—vase, water and all!

'And *that* to you, Wyatt Burns!' she sneered aloud, then scurried out, closing the door silently behind her and fleeing to her own quarters. She lay down to rest and gloat, but not before she had activated the heavy drawbolts on the door in case Wyatt's temper proved as vivid as she feared.

Her hour's rest came and went, and Justine finally had to return to her kitchen duties unrefreshed. She should have been able to sleep, but hadn't. And it wasn't only that she had lain there expecting some immediate reaction from Wyatt. That was only a small part of the problem.

She felt guilty! Not, of course, to Wyatt; he didn't deserve such sentiment. But those lovely flowers surely had deserved a better fate.

But it was far too late to change her mind, even if she had managed the opportunity for a second skulking visit to Wyatt's office. He had already got her message, and let her know it when he stalked silently through the kitchens, glowering at anyone who so much as dared smile at him. For Justine he hadn't even a glower; he turned her own attitude back on her by simply ignoring her completely.

Her work that evening wasn't quickened by compliments from the restaurant or invitations from its owner and his friends. It was plain hard slogging all the way, with what seemed an inordinate number of fumbles by staff and complaints or changes of mind from the customers. The only blessing was Wyatt's total absence from the preserves of her kitchen.

Justine slept late on Sunday, but on awakening she decided it was a day worthy of a drive. Somewhere . . . anywhere . . . so long as it would get her away from Wyatt's and Wyatt until she couldn't avoid him that evening.

Slipping into jeans and a T-shirt, she quietly let herself out and descended the back staircase to the garage. The small car started immediately—a good sign, she thought. Then she put it into reverse and listened in horror as it thumped and bumped its way backward a few feet. She didn't have to be told.

'Oh . . . no!' she moaned when she got out and inspected the flat tire—and no choice but to change it if she was to drive in to meet Peter and Sue for dinner that evening.

Within fifteen minutes Justine had grease all over her fingers, a smudge on her forehead and another across the bridge of her nose, but thank goodness her T-shirt was spared and the tire was changed.

Now all that remained was to get in the car, spend half the afternoon trying to find an open service station to repair the puncture, and perhaps get back in time to change for dinner. It was that, she decided, or take a taxi into the city and be left with no excuse for avoiding the return trip with Wyatt. And *that* she would avoid at all costs.

She was standing there, wiping futilely at her greasy fingers with a scrap of rag, when Wyatt himself stepped into the wide-open car door of the garage.

'More car troubles?' He asked the question casually and without bothering to preface it with any form of greeting.

'Nothing I can't handle,' Justine retorted with quite unnecessary tartness. Stupid man! Did he think she walked around covered in grease all the time?

Wyatt, however, blithely ignored her sour temper.

'Do you suppose you can spare me ten minutes when you've cleaned up?' he asked. 'I know it's your day off, but this involves something I'd like to finish off today, if I can manage it.'

Justine seethed, then shrugged. What was ten minutes anyway . . . she'd spend more than that getting her tyre fixed. 'All right. I'll be in your office in about fifteen minutes,' she replied, and turned to walk away without giving him a chance to reply.

When Justine arrived, he was seated behind his desk looking grimmer than usual, and he hardly looked up as she walked into the room and seated herself without being asked.

'First things first,' he said. 'I've ordered a cab for you to be here at seven. I'd think it appropriate that you be ready.'

'I don't think I understand,' Justine replied, although she thought she understood only too well.

Wyatt looked up smartly, his eyes cold, and she was surprised to notice the dark circles beneath them, suggestive of either late nights or poor sleeping.

'I should think it's pretty damned clear,' he said. 'There will be a taxi here at seven to take you to our dinner engagement.'

'And how do I get home—walk?' she sneered. 'No, thank you; I'll take my own car.'

'That bucket of bolts isn't fit to be driven anywhere,' he snapped. 'I don't want you stranded in the middle of the highway like you were last weekend.'

'It's a perfectly good car,' Justine replied. 'And what's more, I don't think it's any of your business how I travel.'

'It is very definitely my business,' he replied. 'It's my understanding that you're to be my companion this evening, and that means I'll be bringing you back myself.'

'Well, it's not *my* understanding,' Justine snorted. 'We happen to be dining together, with the same people and at the same time. That does not make me your *companion*, and I'll provide my own transportation, thank you.'

'By God, but you're a stubborn woman, Justine,' he sighed. 'But all right . . . please yourself.'

The capitulation was too quick, too easy. It left Justine off balance. So did the way he sat there, silent, and stared at her as if she had two heads.

'Is that all?' she asked at last. She intended to say more, but halted at the shake of his head.

Wyatt thrust a handful of papers across the desk, quickly pulling back his hand as if to remain uncontaminated by her touch as she reached out to take the invoices.

'I presume you can explain all these, since your signature's on them,' he growled.

'I should certainly hope so,' she snapped. Then she looked at the invoices. And looked again. All of them involved large butcher's orders, from the original Wyatt's butcher—the one she had tried to dismiss. And while all of them held her signature, or what appeared to be her signature, none of the quantities involved made any sense at all.

Mystified, she flicked quickly through the invoices, then went through them more slowly. The quantities and prices were astounding. Worse, they were things she would never have approved in a million years.

It took a moment to sink in, but when she looked at the dates, realisation struck her like a thunderclap. Gloria! All the invoices were for the three-week period of Wyatt's American trip, when sheer pressure of work had forced Justine to relinquish the accounting almost entirely to Gloria.

'I'm waiting.' Wyatt's voice was a soft, threatening whisper.

What could she say? To blatantly accuse Gloria without any sort of proof was folly. But to meekly accept the responsibility for . . . this was a worse folly in the long run.

'I . . . I don't know what to say,' Justine faltered. 'I'll have to do some checking.'

'By that I presume you recognise the wrongness of the situation?' he asked, and his voice was grim, horribly grim.

'Yes,' she said. 'Yes, I do. But I can't explain it now, because I don't know how this . . . happened.'

'But it is your signature on these invoices?'

'It certainly looks like it, but I'm . . . not sure,' she replied hesitantly. Was it? Had she somehow been tricked into signing the invoices for payment. Was Gloria that good a forger? Ridiculous, but could it be possible?

Wyatt sighed heavily and his eyes, when he looked at Justine, were sullen with suspicion. How could they be else? she thought. On the face of it, she was next best thing to a thief.

'Right! Leave it for now and go off and get your car fixed up,' he said. 'And you'll kindly leave this to *me* to sort out . . . all right?'

'Oh . . . but . . .' She got no further.

'I said you'll leave it to *me*,' he roared. 'Now kindly get out of here before I lose my temper entirely!'

Justine shivered at the violence in his voice and stance. And she went, exactly as he'd ordered.

Once she was out of the room, however, Wyatt's orders about leaving things to him were tossed off like so much bad advice.

Fine for him to talk, but it was on Justine's shoulders that the blame for the situation had obviously fallen. And since she alone knew who was really to blame, it was quite obviously up to her to ascertain the facts.

Easier said than done, however, since Gloria was nowhere to be found. Justine tried Gloria's quarters, then prowled the restaurant and surrounding grounds, but without success.

Finally she had to give up the attempt and drove into the city in search of a tire repair. She would find Gloria and confront her at the earliest opportunity, but at this precise point in time, ensuring her own independence was of marginally greater significance.

What with one thing and another, it was nearly five o'clock when Justine got back to Wyatt's, and her first move after garaging the car was to resume her search for Gloria. This time she had slightly better success. Armand, whom she found lounging in the last of the evening sunshine, said he had seen Gloria drive away at about two o'clock, but he had also seen her return only half an hour before.

'She must be here somewhere,' he said, 'at least if her car is an indication.' And indeed, Gloria's small sports car was now parked in the staff lot. Justine couldn't remember if it had been there when she herself had left, but it didn't matter now, provided she could find Gloria.

She couldn't be with Wyatt; his luxury car had been taken from the garage and Justine could only assume he was already on his way to his earlier meeting.

The kitchens? It didn't seem logical, but since Gloria wasn't in her quarters or the office she usually used, it was at least a place to start looking.

And a good place, since the first person she encountered as she approached her own little office nook was Gloria herself. The surprise was the warm welcome she received from the dark-haired woman.

'Justine! Oh, I'm so glad you're here. I thought we might have to wait until tomorrow to straighten up this horrible misunderstanding about the butcher,' she said brightly. 'I just left Wyatt a few minutes ago . . . well, perhaps it was more like half an hour . . . and he was *not* amused, let me tell you.'

'So I gathered,' Justine began, only to be cut off as Gloria continued.

'But once I'd explained it all to him, there was no

problem at all, of course. I've just now been making
sure the records are as they should be.'

For the first time, Justine noticed that Gloria was
actively engaged in going through Justine's own records, and her first reaction was one of vivid suspicion.

'Now that you've pacified Wyatt, perhaps you
wouldn't mind explaining it all to me as well,' she suggested. And although she hid her concern, it was there.
The whole story sounded much too smooth for her
liking.

Gloria's eyes narrowed in thought, but when she
spoke up it was in most agreeable tones.

'Oh, but of course,' she said. 'Better than that, I'll
show you, provided you've got five minutes to spare.'
And then, taking Justine's nod as acceptance, she said,
'Right then, let's go along to the cool room.'

Justine followed, wondering as they went just what
the cool room could have to do with meat orders from
nearly a month ago.

She was about to ask when they reached the cool
room, but Gloria already had the huge, heavy door
open and the light turned on inside.

'It's in that far left corner, I think,' she said, waving
at Justine to precede her inside the chilly interior of
the enormous walk-in refrigerator.

Justine walked to the spot where Gloria was point-
ing, but saw nothing that explained anything at all to
her. Indeed, there was nothing there at all but some
layers of cheesecloth taken from some of the large
cheeses in which the restaurant specialised.

Justine turned to ask Gloria what she was talking
about, but her eyes met only the inside sheathing of
the door as it closed.

'Gloria?' she said tentatively. 'Gloria? What are you
doing, for God's sake?'

Her only answer was sudden, Stygian blackness as
the lights were turned off from outside.

CHAPTER NINE

JUSTINE'S first reaction, surprising even to herself, was not panic. The thought of panic, perhaps, but not the panic itself.

Confusion, definitely, however. And a tinge of fear as well, since it was like being plunged into an icy pool of ink. She was blind and virtually deaf as well, even her own tentative movements smothered by the even hum of the refrigerating motors.

What game was Gloria up to? It had to be a game, she thought. Nobody would deliberately shut another person into a cool room—or at least not for long. The constant four-degree temperature (what was that in fahrenheit? she wondered), while of course not as dangerous as the minus twenty in a deep freeze unit, would become dangerously uncomfortable all too soon.

Of course Gloria would open the door very soon. It *must* be some sort of sick joke.

But the door didn't open, and Justine's wonder quickly gave way to concern as she suddenly felt herself growing chilled in the just-above-freezing temperature.

'Gloria?' She started at the sound of her own voice echo rebounding from the insulated walls. 'Gloria?' Louder, this time, which made for louder echoes but was no more effective.

Justine hovered for an instant on the brink of panic, then fought for self-control in the blind darkness and won. Of course! She wasn't locked in. All she had to do was find the door and she could let herself out.

'Find the door.' She said it aloud and almost screamed at the sheer futility of it. But the words echoed over and over in her mind as she gingerly reached out to touch the wall, a wall so familiar in the light but now a strange, evil, clammy coldness.

Inch by inch, a step by faltering step, Justine manoeuvred herself along the frigid walls of the cool room. She nearly screamed once when her shoulder brushed against something hanging there in the darkness. Her mind said it was only the chilled and cooling carcase of a lamb, but her imagination laughed in derision and gave the object more sinister connotations.

She shivered, as much from the cold inside her as the cold outside. Shivered, and continued in her blind, fumbling route around the edge of the room.

'I'm not afraid of the dark,' she said aloud. 'I'm not ... I'm not ... I'm not ... I'm not afraid ...'

She had almost convinced herself when her fingers encountered the corner, moved a bit to her left and touched the edge of the door itself.

Justine's sigh of relief was premature. Totally disorientated as she was by the complete, unrelenting darkness, her searching, numbed fingers couldn't find the latch.

She reached higher, then lower, and finally stretched out both arms, feeling with growing desperation where she thought to find the long, protruding knob that would allow her to escape.

And finally, she did. Her fingers gripped the plunger in a virtual death-grip as she strove to steady her breathing.

At last! Holding firm to the plunger, she flexed her fingers, located the heel of her hand against the frigid metal, and pushed.

It moved! Justine felt it move, felt the snick of the latch being forced, but the door didn't open. Startled, she shoved again, harder this time. And again the latch snicked in vain, the plunger driven home to the extent of its length but to no effect.

Now she *was* frightened. This wasn't anything like

her earlier experience in the cool room. That time the plunger had refused to work, there had been no significant, unmistakable snick as it freed the latch. And that time she hadn't been in blinding darkness!

Justine began to shiver even more. Fear began to build up like an icy stalactite inside her as she pushed at the plunger again and again and again.

'Gloria!' She screamed out the name, oblivious now to the ghostly, frigid echoes that shared her prison. 'Gloria!'

She thumped on the door with her clenched fists, kicked at it with her feet until she stubbed her toe and almost fell. Gloria *must* be out there. She *had* to be.

But if she weren't? Justine's mind shrieked at the thought. It could easily be the next morning before anyone would have the remotest reason to open the cool room. The next morning? More like noon, when Possum just *might* decide on an early start to her apprentices' dinner.

'I'll freeze to death by then,' Justine said aloud.

Her own voice set off the panic; suddenly she was flailing at the door, bruising both hands and feet as she struggled and hit and kicked. Until she once again stubbed her toe, and this was one time too many.

In the darkness, her balance was awry. She fell heavily and felt the thwack as her head struck the concrete of the floor. Then she felt nothing, not even the cold as it gradually left the concrete and flowed up to replace the heat in her flaccid body . . .

Awareness came abruptly; awareness and a startling sensation of being smothered, of being wrapped in a stifling, hot cocoon with something chafing at the edges of it.

Justine's eyes flew open, then closed again immediately at the frightening brightness of the light around her. Then memory flooded in and she opened her eyes again in slits as she tried vainly to move her arms.

'Lie still!' A voice, gruff and alive with tension. Wyatt's voice! She tried again to move, flinging her shoulders around but unable to do anything more. Her head hurt terribly.

'I said lie still.' She could see him, now, crouched beside her. No, not crouched. He was sitting with her legs across his lap and his rippling shoulders . . .

'Stop that,' she said as awareness told her he was rubbing roughly at her legs with something . . . no, not something, a blanket. The same blanket, she thought, that was wrapped so tightly about her arms and shoulders.

'Can you feel your feet?' What a stupid question, she thought. Of course she could. Or could she?

And suddenly she could. Not only feet, but her legs as well. They felt as if a thousand needles were being driven into them, a thousand cats raking her limbs with their claws.

'Oh, please stop it!' she cried. 'It hurts!'

'Good,' he replied, and continued his vigorous chafing, driving the needles deeper, stirring the cats to a frenzy.

Justine tried to kick free of him, but her legs were devoid of muscle power. Her brain commanded motion, but her numbed body denied it. She closed her eyes and sank back against the pillow, weakened by the simple effort of keeping her head up.

'Damn! Possum! Where the hell is that doctor?' Wyatt's voice, ragged and hoarse and husky, boomed in her ears, and Justine winced.

'. . . just coming now,' was the faint, partial reply, and Justine wondered what doctor . . . and why? Then she remembered, and surged upright once again, wild-eyed this time as panic forced aside reality.

For one screaming instant she was once again in that black hell of a cool room, smothered by the darkness, chilled by it. She screamed, a soundless, terrifying scream of pure panic.

Then Wyatt's arms were round her shoulders, his voice soft as honey in her ears. 'It's all right, Justine. You're safe now, my love ... safe ... safe ... safe ... safe ...'

That one word echoed as she slipped away into unconsciousness, but it was the word *love* that blazoned forth like a star when she woke eventually again. Had he really said that? She wanted so very much to believe it, but she couldn't trust her memory.

This time there was no blaze of light to offend her eyes. Only a soft, gentle glow of moonlight over her bed. Her bed ... her room. She was at home. More important, she was warm again, almost *too* warm.

Drowsily, she shifted against the heavy covers, tried to move first her left arm, then her right. It wasn't until she felt the clasp of fingers upon hers that she reared upright. Wyatt! Even in the darkness there was no mistaking his unique presence, the strangely calming melody of his voice.

'Softly, love. You've had a nasty bang on the head,' he said, almost in a whisper. 'But it's okay now. You're safe and in one piece. Are you warm enough? Everywhere? Can you feel your feet now, your legs?'

'I ... I think so,' she replied in a whisper as soft as his own. 'How ... did I get here?'

'I carried you.' There was a strange tremor to his voice, and Justine twisted so she could see his face. But in the misty light his eyes were only dark pools against the whiteness of his features.

'You ... stuck me with needles ... cat claws,' she said, memory erratically emerging from the hazy tunnel of sleep.

He chuckled, a friendly soft sound that comforted her for some reason. 'I had to rub your legs pretty hard to try and get you warm again,' he told her.

'I am warm,' she said. 'But so weak. Why am I so weak?' In her own ears it was a child's voice, a plaintive, lost voice she could hardly recognise as her own.

'Because you damned near froze to death,' he said in a voice that was ragged but still gentle, soft against her ears. 'And the doctor's given you a sedative to help you sleep. I've another one for your head if you think you need it.'

'My . . . head?' She tried to free her hand from his gentle grasp, then left it there and used the other to touch weakly at the back of her crown. There was a large and tender lump there, but not much pain. Justine winced, nonetheless, as she touched it.

'Poor love,' he said. 'Does it hurt very much?'

'Only . . . a little,' she replied. Her eyes were tired, her senses only half aware of their existence. But a part of her was very much alert. 'Why do you call me that?' she asked.

'What?' he enquired, and she knew that he already understood the question.

'Don't . . . tease me, please, Wyatt,' she whispered.

'Does it bother you that I call you . . . love?' he asked. And didn't wait for a reply. 'I certainly hope not, because I don't intend to stop. Unless you want me to.'

Justine said nothing. Something had gone from their relationship. There were no sparks between them, no fire of anger and hatred and revenge. All that had somehow been burned out of her in the icy fires of the cool room. All she had left now was love. But dared she tell him?

'I . . . I thought you hated me,' she said. 'You didn't want to hire me, to have me here . . . or . . . anything.'

Again he chuckled, a warm, friendly sound, gentle as his grip on her right hand. 'I was afraid of you,' he said. What a ridiculous thing; how could anyone be afraid of her? And she must have smiled, because his fingers tightened their grip just a bit before he spoke again.

'Don't laugh; it's quite true. I knew as soon as I saw

you that if you stayed I'd fall in love with you. In fact I suppose I fell in love with you right then . . . I don't know.'

Justine's heart raced. Could it possibly be true?

Wyatt sighed. 'But of course you don't believe me, and I don't blame you a bit. God, but I've treated you horribly! The whole thing started going wrong right from the start, and now . . . now this. I'd have shot myself if you'd been badly hurt, because the whole damned thing has been my fault. It wouldn't have happened at all if I weren't so stupid.'

'Wasn't you,' Justine replied muzzily. 'It was Gloria. You weren't even here.'

'It was Gloria who locked you up in the cold room, but it was me that set you up for it,' he replied, running his free hand angrily through his hair. Now that her eyes had adjusted to the soft light, Justine could see how tired he looked, how the deep lines had gathered beneath his eyes and beside his mouth.

He reached out then to brush his fingers across her cheek, a touch like angel's breath. 'Are you sure you want to hear all this now?' he asked. 'You should be resting, really.'

'I'm fine,' Justine whispered. 'I'll rest better when you've told me everything. And so will you, I hope. You look terrible, Wyatt, as if you haven't slept for days.'

He laughed softly. 'Just less than one day, really. It's almost dawn on Monday.'

'Monday! That means I've slept . . .'

'Only the better part of twelve hours,' he said. 'And too much of that was on the bloody cold floor of the cool room. God! I've never been so afraid in my life as I was when I found you there.'

'H-how did you find me?'

'In a minute,' he said. 'I've got to start at the very beginning or I'll miss something, and I want you to understand. All right?'

At her nod, he continued. 'I think I told you the chef you replaced had been playing silly little games of his own with the books. Well, I knew he had help, and right from the start I suspected Gloria, but I couldn't prove it and didn't want to try until I was sure I'd catch her out. I was . . . using my rather questionable masculine charms to . . . keep her attentions diverted.'

Justine grinned at that, especially when he was forced to add, rather shamefaced, that perhaps he'd used them a bit too well.

'And then you came along and really put everything at sixes and sevens, because I was fast falling in love with you, but I didn't have the proof I needed about Gloria, and I was just vain enough to believe I could handle both of you,' he said. 'Lord, Justine, you've led me a merry chase. I thought I'd go mad. I was jealous of Armand; I would have strangled Peter last weekend if I'd got my hands on him. Even being off on that junket to America didn't help. I kept wanting to phone, just to hear your voice. But at least that trip did accomplish something; it led Gloria into thinking she could carry on her little game with that crooked butcher—and she did. You saw the invoices.'

'Yesterday.' Was it only that long ago? she thought. It seemed like forever, now that her ordeal was over and she was safe.

'Yesterday, yes. And when I confronted you with it, I knew damned well you had nothing to do with it. I was just so . . . so frustrated and angry at your treatment of me, your refusal to let me apologise. I wanted to strike back.'

He sighed, more heavily than before. 'God, I doubt if you'll ever forgive me,' he muttered. 'Anyway, as soon as you'd gone I dragged Gloria in here and confronted *her*, and of course she couldn't get out of it. Maybe she didn't try, I don't know. Anyway, she admitted everything finally and I gave her two hours to get out and never come back. She was angry, fair

enough, but I never thought she'd try anything like
. . . like what she did.'

He stopped for a moment then, and looked at her
very seriously. And guiltily. 'The next bit's not easy to
talk about,' he said. 'I should be horribly ashamed,
but I'm not, because partly it's why I was able to find
you so quickly.'

Now it was Justine's turn to squeeze his hand gently.
'Just tell me,' she coaxed. 'I . . . don't feel very vengeful
right now.' And I love you, she thought, but for some
inane reason she couldn't put it in words. Not yet.

'Well, I hung about until you got back yesterday.
You didn't see my car because I hid it; I wanted you
to think I'd gone. And then I did go, damn it! If I'd
just stayed another fifteen minutes none of this would
have happened. I got my other business done and was
right on time to meet Peter and Sue. They'll be along
to see you this afternoon, by the way; I've already let
them know you're okay. But last night, when you
didn't take the cab I'd sent for you, and nobody could
find you, I came straight back immediately.'

'But why would you do that?' Justine asked. 'I mean,
we agreed I was going to take my own car. Surely you
must have . . .'

'Damned independent wench,' he grinned. 'I knew
you thought you were going to take your own car;
that's why I hung about until you got back and how I
knew something was wrong. Your car was still in the
garage, just as I'd planned. Couldn't go very far with
two flat tires.'

Justine gasped. 'You mean you . . .?'

'Guilty! I figured you wouldn't notice until it was
too late, and by then the cab I'd ordered would be
there and you'd take it, forcing you—of course—to
return with me.'

'That's . . . that's . . .' She was quite lost for words.
In fact, she couldn't even quite conceive of Wyatt
Burns going to such devious extremes.

'Dirty, rotten, underhanded, devious . . . and desperate!' he said with a grin that was nowhere near as guilty as it should have been. 'Well, what was I supposed to do? You wouldn't talk to me. You threw away any peace-offering I made. Oh, God, Justine! I honestly thought I'd completely destroyed any chance I might ever have had with that performance here in this bed. I . . . I was so damned jealous, at the time . . . and then to find that I'd been falsely accusing you, which of course I should have known anyway. I was just out of my head.'

'Forget that for now,' she said. 'What happened last night?'

'Well, the cabbie phoned me, and I got worried right away, so I had him rouse Armand for me, and by the time I got here after the fastest drive *ever* from downtown Sydney, he'd already searched most of the place. But neither of us ever even thought of the cool room; we didn't realise what had really happened, of course. We thought you'd been taken ill, or . . . oh, God, I don't know what we thought.

'And then Armand mentioned the cool room, but he said the latch had been repaired, and of course it had. Still, I thought it best to check, and when I saw it was latched from the *outside*——!'

For the first time, he released Justine's fingers, and buried his face in both hands as he breathed heavily to try and hold back the shudders of anger.

It seemed to take forever, but finally he looked up and his eyes were bleak with suppressed anger. 'I swear I'll get Gloria for this,' he growled. 'If it's the last thing I ever do, I'll . . .'

'You'll do nothing of the sort,' Justine replied in a voice that took on strength from somewhere inside her. She reached out to capture his hand, holding it tightly.

'Don't you see?' she said. 'Revenge is a wasted emotion, a destructive emotion. It doesn't solve anything, it only makes things worse. It was revenge that made me lead you on about Peter, and ... oh ... everything. Forget Gloria; she just isn't important any more.'

Suddenly she was so very tired again. Wyatt was talking, but his words were only a comforting drone as she drifted away into a peaceful oblivion that took her from the darkness into the full light of day.

Justine's eyes had no great problem when she woke, however, because somebody—Wyatt?—had thoughtfully closed the curtains over the windows. It was brighter than when last she'd wakened, but only marginally.

She reached back to finger the bump on her crown and was hardly surprised to find it quite as large as she remembered. If that was true, then everything else she remembered might also be true. It seemed hard to believe that Wyatt had sat there, in the middle of the night, holding her hand and talking to her without any of their usual clashing.

She looked over at her bedside clock. Eleven o'clock! At first tentatively, then with growing confidence, she slid her legs from under the high-piled sheets and blankets and stood upright.

Naked, she padded slowly into the bathroom and for the first time since her ordeal she got a good look at herself. 'My God!' she muttered at the reflected image of smudged make-up and tangled hair.

Her arms and legs felt tender, as if the skin had been rubbed against something rough. Justine grinned at herself in the mirror. What had Wyatt used to chafe her? she wondered. Certainly something much rougher than the blanket she remembered.

She looked longingly at the shower stall, wondering if her current feeling of well-being was only temporary. Did she dare risk the shower she so desired? Another look at her hair made the decision irrelevant. She didn't dare *not* risk it.

Moments later she was revelling in the smell of

shampoo and the gentle laving of warm water over her body. It would be wonderful, she thought, to just lie down on the floor of the shower and stay there until the hot water ran out.

A brisk knock at the bathroom door interrupted that reverie, and Justine returned to normal and the sound of Wyatt's deep voice.

'Justine! Are you all right in there?' There was concern in his voice, and she felt herself go even warmer at the thought of it. Maybe he really *had* said he loved her.

'I'm fine,' she called. 'I'm just taking a shower.'

His next words were louder, and she realised he'd opened the bathroom door and was in there with her. And angry.

'Are you right out of your tree? My God, woman! You can't just hop out of a sickbed and . . . and take a bloody shower. Suppose you had a relapse and fell, or something.'

'I feel fine.' And she did, too. More than fine, in fact, she felt deliciously clean, and warm and right with the world.

'I've brought you up some warm soup.' No anger now; his voice was soft, gentle, almost paternal.

Justine giggled. Warm soup! How sick did he think she was? 'I don't want any warm soup,' she replied through the pebble-glass screen. 'I'm hungry.'

There was a silence, then, 'Well what do you want?'

'Hang on a minute and I'll think about it while I wash my hair,' she replied. He answered, but she was already under the plunging spray, gently sudsing in shampoo and trying to avoid the bump on her head as she massaged her scalp.

When she finally emerged and could hear again, there was silence from outside the shower stall. She had to call out, 'Wyatt?' before he replied.

'Of course I'm still here. Do you think I'd dare leave you alone in here?'

'Well, you're going to have to in a minute. I'm nearly done,' she said.

'You mean you don't want me to wash your back?' There was a mild chuckle in the question; he was pulling her leg, she thought. And wondered what he'd do if she said yes.

'I wouldn't mind,' she whispered, as much to herself as anything else. But he heard; she knew it by the sharply indrawn breath.

Then: 'I . . . don't think I'd better. Look, will you hurry up and get out of there; I'm worried about you.'

'Spoilsport!' She didn't try to subdue that comment. He was a spoilsport. Why couldn't he stop being so serious and just do as she asked?

'I'm not a spoilsport,' he replied. 'I just don't want to start anything I haven't got time to finish. Peter and Sue are waiting to see you, and they won't wait for ever.'

'Oh . . . goody!' she cried. 'I like Peter and Sue, they're nice.'

Wyatt's oath was muffled in the motion as he suddenly slammed open the shower stall door and bodily lifted her out, oblivious to the water that cascaded over him in the process.

'Stupid woman!' he muttered. 'I knew it; you're still in shock.' And before she could protest he had lifted her in his arms, carried her back to the bed and was gently but firmly towelling her dry.

'I'm all right,' she complained peevishly. Wyatt ignored her until he had her sitting up and well tucked under the blankets.

'Now don't you move,' he snapped in tones that denied any argument. 'Dammit, Justine, you *worry* me. Now you're going to sit there and eat this soup if I have to pour it down you!'

She resisted him for the first few bites, but as the warmth and nourishment settled into her stomach, some of her hysteria faded. Soon she was much calmer, indeed almost shy after her earlier exuberance. She tried to tell him, but he shook his finger at her and demanded she finish the soup first.

'I'm ... sorry,' she was finally allowed to say. 'I guess I was getting a little ... silly?'

'A *lot* silly.' His face was deadpan sober, but his eyes laughed at her. Nice eyes, gentle, comforting eyes. 'It comes from too much exercise on an empty stomach.'

Justine looked away shyly, but he reached out and gently turned her head back. 'Why didn't you tell me that you'd phoned last week when your car broke down?'

'You didn't ask,' she lied. And then, 'But how did you know?'

He grinned. 'It was just one of the things that came out when Gloria was bidding me a fond farewell. I suppose you want to know what she was doing in my suite at that time of night?'

'Not really,' she said, lying again and even more strongly this time. Then, suddenly, she realised it *wasn't* a lie. Whatever the reason, she knew it wouldn't matter and never had.

'That's good,' he replied, 'because I honestly don't know either. I know where *I* was—downstairs waiting for you.'

Justine once again had that ridiculous mental picture of Wyatt waiting on the steps like a distraught parent. 'You weren't,' she chuckled.

'I damned well was! I'm beginning to think I've been waiting for you all my life,' he said, and his voice was tender as he reached up to run his fingers along her cheek.

'Well, considering how I look at the moment, that has to be a compliment,' Justine smiled. 'Now that I've finished the soup, do you suppose it would be all right for me to dry my hair and get some clothes on?'

'Definitely not! The doctor said you were to stay in bed until he came for another check on you.'

'Well, he's not going to see me looking like this,' Justine replied adamantly. 'Lord, he'd have me in bed for a week!'

Wyatt's reply was to bring her a huge towel from the bathroom and her hairbrush and comb. 'Right, sit up here and I'll do your hair for you,' he said. 'And no arguments. You'll stay in that bed until the doctor comes if I have to come in with you to make sure of it.'

He dried her hair gently, considerate of the lump on her crown, then his skilled fingers moved softly through it, sorting and sifting out the tangles much more gently than she could have done it herself. Justine closed her eyes and let herself relax completely, revelling in his touch.

'You're in the wrong business,' she sighed. 'You should have been a hairdresser.'

Wyatt chuckled. 'Well, I might consider it ... provided the price was right.' And he stopped brushing to run his fingers in a sensual track down her cheek and neck.

Justine shivered, but it wasn't the shiver of being cold. If anything she was too warm. And getting warmer, she found as his lips followed the path of his fingers.

'Don't you want to know the price?' he whispered, gently turning her so that his lips could reach her mouth.

'I'm not sure; I doubt if I'd be able to afford it,' she whispered when he finally stopped kissing her.

'Of course you will,' he breathed. 'You're going to marry a rich man, aren't you?'

'Am I?' The question was hardly more than a sigh as the covers slipped from her when he turned her completely into his arms.

'Just as soon as I can arrange it,' he said. 'I've waited far too long already, my love.'

'So have I,' she whispered into his waiting lips. 'Oh, Wyatt, so have I!'

Harlequin® Plus

BROWN BETTY
AND OTHER STRANGE FOODS

A restaurant such as Wyatt's, which specializes in old-fashioned English cooking, is bound to have a menu consisting of some very peculiar-looking items—to our North American eyes, at least. Listed below are a few quaintly named British dishes and drinks along with our attempts to tell you just what they are.

Brown Betty	a strong ale mixed with brown sugar, water, lemon, cloves, cinnamon and brandy and served hot, afloat with a piece of brown nutmeg-sprinkled toast
Brown Windsor	a thick beef broth
Bubble and Squeak	leftover greens and potatoes, fried with bacon (name comes from the hissing sound of frying bacon grease)
Cock-a-Leekie Soup	a hot chicken-and-leek soup
Flummery	a pudding made from oatmeal, water and sugar, served with crushed fruit and cream
Fool	a dessert consisting of cold fruit purée, laced with cream
Maids of Honor	custard-filled tarts
Sally Lun	a golden-crusted round bun
Spotted Dick	a pudding with raisins or currants
Stargazy Pie	a pie of whole small fish, such as herrings, arranged like spokes of a wheel with heads turned toward outside edge; top pastry doesn't cover heads, allowing the fish eyes to gaze at the stars
Syllabub	a dessert consisting of a well-whipped mixture of wine, cream, sugar and brandy
Welsh Rabbit (or Rarebit)	a dish consisting of cheese, with small amounts of milk, butter, egg and flour, cooked and served over toast.

Legacy of
PASSION

BY CATHERINE KAY

A love story begun long ago comes full circle...

Venice, 1819: Contessa Allegra di Rienzi, young, innocent, unhappily married. She gave her love to Lord Byron—scandalous, irresistible English poet. Their brief, tempestuous affair left her with a shattered heart, a few poignant mementos—and a daughter he never knew about.

Boston, today: Allegra Brent, modern, independent, restless. She learned the secret of her great-great-great-grandmother and journeyed to Venice to find the di Rienzi heirs. There she met the handsome, cynical, blood-stirring Conte Renaldo di Rienzi, and like her ancestor before her, recklessly, hopelessly lost her heart.

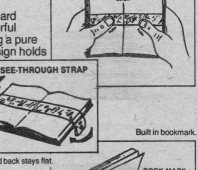

Harlequin Romances

The books that let you escape
into the wonderful world of romance!
Trips to exotic places...interesting
plots...meeting memorable people...
the excitement of love.... These are
integral parts of Harlequin Romances—
the heartwarming novels read by
women everywhere.

Many early issues are now available.
Choose from this great selection!

Choose from this list of Harlequin Romance editions.*

*Some of these book were originally published under different titles.

Relive a great love story...
with Harlequin Romances
Complete and mail this coupon today!

Harlequin Reader Service

In the U.S.A.
1440 South Priest Drive
Tempe, AZ 85281

In Canada
649 Ontario Street
Stratford, Ontario N5A 6W2

Please send me the following Harlequin Romance novels. I am enclosing my check or money order for $1.50 for each novel ordered, plus 75¢ to cover postage and handling.

☐ 975	☐ 1157	☐ 1171	☐ 1190	☐ 1226
☐ 978	☐ 1158	☐ 1174	☐ 1193	☐ 1228
☐ 991	☐ 1159	☐ 1176	☐ 1197	☐ 1233
☐ 1150	☐ 1164	☐ 1178	☐ 1199	☐ 1246
☐ 1152	☐ 1165	☐ 1182	☐ 1211	☐ 1494
☐ 1154	☐ 1166	☐ 1189	☐ 1212	☐ 1605

Number of novels checked @ $1.50 each = $_____

N.Y. and Ariz. residents add appropriate sales tax. $_____

Postage and handling $_____ .75

TOTAL $_____

I enclose _____
(Please send check or money order. We cannot be responsible for cash sent through the mail.)

Prices subject to change without notice.

NAME _____
(Please Print)

ADDRESS _____
(APT. NO.)

CITY _____

STATE/PROV. _____

ZIP/POSTAL CODE _____

Offer expires August 31, 1983

30256000000